A BITTER DECISION . . .

Prickles of apprehension ran up Elizabeth's spine. She unclenched her hands from the edge of Wynmalen's desk and slowly rubbed her arms as if they were cold. Her eyes were wide.

Wynmalen steeled himself against those eyes. Those eyes he'd once thought a man could drown in . . .

"I have decided that you would make a most excellent wife for Anthony, Miss Chanders." He felt his teeth clench. . . . Hastily he added, "I am sure you are quite willing to oblige me in this."

He had not spoken quickly enough. Before his sentence was finished, Elizabeth had cried, "You can't be serious!"

Jove titles by Christina Cordaire

HEART'S DECEPTION
LOVE'S TRIUMPH

Coming in September 1993

PRIDE'S FOLLY

Love's Triumph

Christina Cordaire

JOVE BOOKS, NEW YORK

LOVE'S TRIUMPH

A Jove Book / published by arrangement with
the author

PRINTING HISTORY
Jove edition / May 1993

ISBN: 0-515-11102-3

Jove Books are published by The Berkley Publishing Group,
200 Madison Avenue, New York, New York 10016.
The name "JOVE" and the "J" logo
are trademarks belonging to Jove Publications, Inc.

PRINTED IN THE UNITED STATES OF AMERICA

10 9 8 7 6 5 4 3 2 1

Love's Triumph

CHAPTER
✽ ONE

Surely she could think of some way to save them! She must, she was the oldest . . . three and twenty this April. Her younger sister Lucinda had always looked to her for guidance and support, and Jonathan . . . their dear little half brother Jonathan had just assumed that she was his mother, almost from the moment he was born.

Elizabeth sighed with such emotion that her horse shifted under her, swinging his head around to look at her.

"It's all right, Socrates." She smoothed a gloved hand down his satiny neck, and he returned to his quiet contemplation of the scene before them.

In the golden meadow below, Lucy rode her dainty mare, leading Jonathan's pony and telling him, "Sit up straight. That's right, dear. My, how nice you look, almost like Father!"

"Really? Oh, do I really look like him, Luce?" He turned his face toward his sister, excitement shining in his eyes. "I should like above all things to look like Father."

"Well then," Lucinda said with mock briskness, "you must face forward and keep . . ."

The rising wind snatched the rest of her words away, and Elizabeth, watching from the knoll, could hear no more. It tugged loose tendrils of her hair, and it chilled the quick tears that came unbidden to her eyes.

Jonathan wanted to be like Father. A father he knew only from the portrait of him, stern in his scarlet regimentals, that hung over the library fireplace. A father that was not even his own, but one he had shifted his love and allegiance to in the face of his own father's indifference. The man in the painting was his mother's first husband—Elizabeth and Lucinda's father.

Well, he could not have found a better man to emulate. Colonel Lord Jason Chanders, Fifth Viscount Chanders, was one of Britain's great heroes.

Now Elizabeth prayed that Jonathan would be like him. Firm and wise, kind and gentle, their father had been all that they could have wished him to be. Not like . . . no, she simply couldn't bear their stepfather's sharing space in the same thought in which she'd remembered her beloved father!

Lucinda called, "Elizabeth! There you are. I didn't see you come back from your gallop." She led Jonathan's pony up the gentle rise to her sister's side. "Was Socrates a good boy for you?"

"Yes, he's always a good boy." Elizabeth returned her sister's warm smile. "Look, dear," she warned. "The wind has shifted, and the sky is darkening over there." She pointed with her crop to where ominous clouds were gathering, roiling with wind and heavy with the promise of rain. "We'd better make for home."

A small voice interrupted, "Shall we have tea in the nursery today, 'Lizbeth, or must I have my tea with only Bess again?" Jonathan struggled manfully to keep the complaint from his voice, and the sisters shot each other a glance full of **understanding** over his shining blond head.

Jonathan spent so much time **locked away** with only his nurse for company. His father, their stepfather, could not bear the sight of him.

Even though the two girls tried hard to understand, they had to make an even greater effort not to feel resentment over the situation. Sir Charles Mainwaring, therefore, was not in their favor.

"Of course we shall have tea with you, Jonathan. It's kind of you to invite us." Elizabeth made the promise, swiftly calculating how early they would have to ask Cook to prepare the nursery tea if they were to be in time for their tea with Sir Charles.

Over Jonathan's head Lucinda sent Elizabeth an approving smile. She understood the necessity for keeping their presence in the nursery a secret from their stepfather, but like Elizabeth, she loathed being devious. But it was the only way they could spend as much time as they did with Jonathan.

There was a low growl of thunder from the dark clouds away to their right. They turned their mounts in that direction and sent them off at a pace that was deliberately slowed to accommodate the pony's.

Elizabeth watched the gathering storm with care. How symbolic that they rode toward it to return to Chandering. Their home had become increasingly a place of tension since the death of their dear mother four years ago, and for some time Elizabeth had been living with the feeling that a storm was about to break *within* the walls of the mansion.

A flurry of leaves, torn green from their branches by a mighty gust, pelted the three, startling the horses.

Jonathan's pony pulled back against the lead and tried to rear. Lucinda cast a frightened glance at her sister. Jonathan clung desperately to his pony's mane, lips set and eyes wide with a fear he'd rather die with than voice.

Elizabeth called over the rising whistle of the wind, "Jonathan, would you mind awfully riding with me?" Even as she spoke, the wind strengthened. "I'm afraid to ask Pony to keep up while carrying such a big boy as you, and we must really hurry or the rain will catch us and we'll all be soaked."

Lucinda gave her sister a warm glance, approving of the saving of the child's manly pride. Then she turned her full attention to her mare. The handsome chestnut she rode was becoming fractious now that she was bound for home and bidden there by the rising wind.

"I should be happy to oblige you, Elizabeth." Jonathan gasped as the pony plunged again. Elizabeth pushed her horse into the pony, limiting its ability to misbehave by trapping it between her sister's mount and her own.

"Sorry," she told Lucinda.

"It's all right," her sister answered breathlessly. "Frankly, I wish you'd trample the little beast." Lucinda gave the pony an exasperated glare as it swung its hindquarters around and tried to kick her mare.

Jonathan reached eager hands up to Elizabeth. Pony was equally eager to run to the barn, and though Jonathan was progressing well in his riding, he knew his skill was limited, and he was more than glad to try for the warmth of home before the storm broke.

Elizabeth swung him up onto her lap, cradled him to her firmly, and they were off for home.

The horses were impatient, aware they were headed for the barn and shelter from the approaching rain.

They shook their manes and champed their bits, but were too well trained to snatch them and run away.

Even Pony was being good now that a frightened little boy wasn't digging his heels into his sleek sides, trying to hang on.

As they swept through the gate posts and pounded up the long drive, Elizabeth thought how appropriate it was to her forebodings that the clouds now hung on the very turrets of Chandering.

Andrews, the head groom, was waiting at the foot of the front steps.

"You should have come earlier, misses. The storm be about to break. You could'a had trouble." He scowled at them and raised an admonishing finger. "Ye'd no need to leave coming home so long!"

"Yes, Andrews," the girls chorused, used to his fussing over their safety and loving him for it. "We're sorry, Andrews."

They each laughed as they heard the other voicing the same words—and in unison. They'd grown up with Andrew's mother-hen clucking and had always answered so.

"Go on with you." Andrews waved them off with mock disapproval and stomped off, leading the horses away, their long tails flying and snapping like banners in the high wind.

The sisters, Jonathan between them, rushed up the broad stairs and through the door Lazenby held open for them.

As the butler closed the huge door behind them, the storm broke in all its fury.

"You have made it just in time, young misses." The tall butler's voice, too, held a note of censure.

Elizabeth and Lucinda exchanged a look, and Elizabeth pressed her lips firmly together. It wouldn't do to offend Lazenby. Lucinda understood that she was the one to speak, and said, "We're sorry to have caused you concern, Lazenby."

"Truly," Elizabeth added.

Jonathan nodded vigorously, and the butler, placated by their contrition, allowed himself the hint of a smile as he stalked majestically back to his duties.

Lucinda and Jonathan scurried up the grand staircase, making for the nursery. Elizabeth headed toward the kitchen to order Jonathan's tea.

As she went, she made a determined effort not to dwell on the fact that Jonathan had merely nodded to Lazenby. More and more she was becoming aware that Jonathan did not speak in this great house . . . not until he gained the sanctuary of the nursery.

As she walked down the smooth stone steps to the kitchen, Elizabeth wondered how long it would be before the strained relationships in the house erupted. And when they did, what she would be able to do about it.

CHAPTER
❖ TWO

"Damn and Blast!" The man, so graceful just a moment before on the back of his huge bay stallion, staggered and let go of the reins to avoid yanking his horse in the mouth. He steadied himself against the granite newel post at the foot of the steps that swept down to the drive and cursed anew the French artillery shell that had wrecked him.

Whimpering, the sleek black mastiff that had run beside the horse thrust his muzzle into the man's hand, offering comfort.

The stallion, uneasy at the anger in his master's tone, skittered away a few strides and snorted. Then he warily stood his ground just out of reach, his ears flicking back and forth restlessly.

"Sorry, old boy." The Earl of Wynmalen, his balance regained, reached for his mount's bridle and smoothed the sweaty neck soothingly. "Sorry, Crytor. It's hellish getting accustomed to being a damned cripple, that's all."

Belatedly a groom arrived to take the huge stallion away. By then the soft-voiced apologies of his master had worked their magic, and Crytor's ears were forward and inquiring again.

"Go with him, Crytor." Wynmalen verbally dismissed the horse, who would otherwise have refused to leave him, and said to the groom, "Be sure to cool him well before you grain him."

"Aye, milord."

Wynmalen limped up the stairs that led to the huge double doors of Castle Wynmalen, his ancestral home. His butler, Stone, swung one of the doors open as he reached them, the dog at his heels.

"I trust Your Lordship had a pleasant journey?" The majordomo's bland tone belied the bright inquiry in his eyes.

"Yes, I found him. It was just as you had hinted. He was . . . immeshed . . . in her toils by the time I arrived. If I'd been a few minutes later, the trap would have been sprung."

Stone smiled his satisfaction.

"I owe you a debt of gratitude, Stone," Wynmalen told him. "So does the young jackanapes, though he little realizes it at present." He pressed a hand to his thigh absently as he spoke. The gesture galvanized his butler.

"There's a hot fire in your study, Your Lordship. I'll bring you your tea there."

"Very well. And send him to me when he comes."

Stone nodded regally, understanding without being told that "him" was the "young jackanapes," Anthony, Lord Stayne.

Their father, the Marquess, was away at the Peace Conference in Vienna. The responsibility of keeping young Lord Anthony from disgracing the family name fell squarely on his older brother's shoulders. It seemed unjust with all else he had to bear.

Stone watched the Earl move away, and shared for a moment the deep concern the Marquess had for his wounded son. Since the death of his lovely Marchioness, his sons had become all that mattered in life to the Marquess. It was enough to break one's heart, seeing the master when the news of the young Earl's misfortune had reached him.

The butler sighed and shook his head. He regretted as sharply as did his master the necessities of duty that kept the Marquess from being here at home with his hero son.

His face full of pity, he watched as Wynmalen, seeking the warmth that would ease the infernal ache in his leg, limped briskly toward his study. His former grace quite gone, the Earl now moved with a lurching gait.

His younger brother arrived half an hour later. Stone opened the study door himself, dismissing the footman there with a curt nod, and stood aside, his attitude as respectful as his eyes were not.

Tony entered and stood just inside the door, waiting for his brother to acknowledge his presence. The huge dog that was his brother's constant companion observed him without stirring.

Wynmalen was studying the portrait that hung above the fireplace. It was a little too large to be hanging there, having been painted originally to grace the library fireplace.

From within the ornate gold-leafed frame, a younger Wynmalen gazed arrogantly out at the world. His face was smooth and still attractive, and he stood straight and tall, the rich scarlet of his uniform glowing softly in the subdued light of the room.

The painted Wynmalen had been exiled to the study by the man who looked up at him—the man who wished to keep visitors to his home from making

awkward comparisons. He despised the portrait because there was no cane at the painted officer's
side—no cane on which to lean when his leg betrayed him. The Wynmalen in the painting was still
whole.

His hand stole up to touch his left cheek. To touch
the hard and shiny scar that slashed across it, lifting
the corner of his mouth in a slight, perpetually cynical
smile.

Tony's face registered his compassion for the tor-
tured thoughts that he knew were passing through his
brother's mind. Then he returned his features to bland
boredom and cleared his throat.

Wynmalen whirled in his seat, anger blossoming in
him.

"So you've finally decided to come, have you?"

Tony answered with a hint of laughter, "I had to
dress, you know."

"Dammit, Tony! Do you really wish to have that
woman hanging beside you in the portrait gallery?"

Tony knew his brother referred to the family tradi-
tion of painting each member of the family and his
spouse in the first year of their marriage. Their like-
nesses were then added to the generations of portraits
already decorating the walls of the long gallery above
the main hall. Still, it was with considerable difficulty
that Tony forbore making the obvious joke about not
wishing to be hanged at all.

"No, Marc. I have no wish to add her to the family."

"Then why the hell were you—"

"Marc, I have never been one to turn down a treat
when it is offered me, and well you know it."

"Yes, to my sorrow. I seem to be spending more and
more of my time extricating you from the conse-
quences of your, er, fondness for treats."

Wynmalen brought his fist down sharply on his desk. "Blast it, Tony, don't you know that the world is full of unscrupulous parents who will stop at nothing to see their daughters married to a title and a healthy fortune?"

"It's a very minor title, Marc."

Wynmalen struggled with his anger at his younger brother's casual treatment of what could have been a scandal. A scandal that would have ended with Tony having to marry a very unsuitable girl.

"Tony, be serious. Your fortune is one of the largest in England, almost as great as my own. And if your title is minor, it is still a title, after all. Besides—have you thought what Father would say?"

"Spare me." Tony sighed. "Marc, you never used to be such a serious chap, but since you have become one"—the blond youth sighed again—"I promise to try to do less to cause you concern."

Marcus Stayne, Earl of Wynmalen, looked at the contrite expression on his brother's face. "I can see I shall have no peace until I have settled you down with some sensible girl."

Tony grimaced. "You wouldn't . . . it sounds like a prison sentence!"

"If I thought there was a steady, sensible girl in all of England over whom I could gain the power to do so, I should frog march you up the aisle to her side and leg-shackle you to her in an instant."

Tony grinned at him, "Thank God there is no such young lady." He looked around, adroitly changing the subject. "Where is Stone with the tea? He lured me here with promises of sustenance."

As if conjured up by the mention of his name, Stone appeared, bearing a large silver waiter with their elaborate tea upon it.

The two men settled themselves near the desk, in tacit agreement that the subject of the younger Lord's indiscretion should temporarily be shelved . . . at least until after their tea.

Chapter

*Three

All during the tea that Elizabeth and Lucinda shared with Jonathan at Chandering, the storm raged. Trees sighed and moaned, battering the ancient walls of the house and clawing at the windows with branches denuded of their tender leaves by the sudden spring gale.

Servants ran everywhere throughout the huge structure, opening windows and striving to drag heavy shutters closed against the wind. By the time the two footmen reached the upper story that housed the nursery, the men were soaked to their waists.

Powdered wigs dripping, they came to attention beside the tea table. Henson, the older of the two, bowed. "With your permission, miss, we'll close the shutters."

"Of course," Elizabeth answered.

"'Lizabeth, they're all wet." Jonathan's eyes were round. "How did they get all wet inside the house?"

"Watch and you will see." Lucinda drew her pretty cashmere shawl more closely around her shoulders when the cool air rushed into the room as the younger footman stretched daringly out of the window to grip the shutters.

It took both men to close and fasten them against the violent force of the wind. Then, all shutters secured, they marched briskly across the nursery and bowed from the doorway.

Before they were quite gone, Elizabeth called out an order. "Go to the kitchen at once. Tell Cook I shall hold her responsible for your being thoroughly dry before you return to your duties."

The younger footman looked his startled thanks, but Henson was used to Miss Elizabeth's caring nature and was able to say, wooden-faced, "Very good, Miss Elizabeth." Then they were gone, closing the door carefully behind them.

Jonathan smiled at Elizabeth. "Now it's really cozy. We can have some more tea."

Lucinda laughed. "You just want more of Cook's scones." She looked pointedly at his cup, more than half milk in deference to his youth, and more than half-cold due to his disinterest in it.

Elizabeth saved him from a reply by saying, "It is much nicer with the shutters closed, isn't it? The smoke stays in the chim—"

The nursery door burst open, and Henson half fell into the room. "Miss Elizabeth," he gasped, winded from taking the stairs three at a time. "He's coming! Sir Charles is on his way *here*."

Jonathan's face crumpled. Lucinda's showed something akin to fear, but Elizabeth's showed only a fierce determination. "Quickly, Bess," she ordered. "Put Jonathan to bed. Henson, take the tea things down the back stairs!"

The plump nurserymaid snatched her young charge from his place and rushed from the room with him.

The footman seized the tea tray and fled the nursery with it clattering.

Elizabeth grabbed her sister's hand and ran to the door.

"*Quickly*, we must be on the floor below before our stepfather arrives there!"

The two girls hurled themselves toward the stairs and ran down, slippered feet flying, to the floor below. There they glanced at each other. Smoothing a curl and replacing a tumbled ribbon, each restored the other to order, just as they heard their stepfather's firm tread in the passage.

Elizabeth shoved her sister into her bedchamber doorway without ceremony, linked arms with her, and pretended they were just leaving that room.

Lucinda understood immediately and began chattering brightly, "So you think my old blue will do for the Foresters' dinner if I have Martha add a new flounce?"

"Yes, indeed. Martha is so clever with her needle, no one will know." Elizabeth felt like a simpleton.

Not even his severest critic could say their stepfather was a nipfarthing. Neither sister had to have flounces added to make a gown do for one more function, and well they knew it. Nevertheless, she gave her sister's arm a little squeeze to congratulate her on her quick wit, and put a surprised look on her own face at encountering Sir Charles.

Sir Charles, suspicion blazing in his handsome face, glared at the girls. "There you are. Why are you late for tea?"

He took a deep breath to steady himself, evidently aware that his anger was at odds with his words, and spoke more calmly. "I have been waiting these ten minutes."

Elizabeth noted his effort with relief. "We were looking over some of Lucinda's gowns and lost track of the time, Sir Charles."

She felt her sister wince at the lie and knew Lucinda

hated the falsehood as much as she herself did. How she wished they could be free of the necessity ever to tell even one! They'd had to lie more than once for Jonathan's sake, but the protection of their baby brother from Sir Charles's rages was more important to her even than the security of her very soul.

What a tangle they were caught in! Sir Charles no less than they, for he could no more help blaming his son Jonathan for the death of his beloved wife than Elizabeth and Lucinda could help despising him for doing so.

"Come then," he said brusquely, turning back to lead them to the drawing room. "The tea is getting cold."

By the time they were all seated in the drawing room, the tea was, indeed, tepid. Elizabeth looked toward her stepfather. "Shall I order more tea? This is, I fear, not quite hot."

"We're sorry, Stepfather," Lucinda blurted, then bit her lip in confusion as he turned to look at her.

"Please call me Sir Charles if you can't bring yourself to call me Father." His voice was crisp with displeasure.

"Yes, Sir Charles," Lucinda said softly, her gaze locked on her hands clasped firmly in her lap to stop herself from wringing them.

Elizabeth looked toward the door, fiercely willing Lazenby to materialize with the tea. She dreaded the scene that was sure to come.

Their stepfather seemed to delight in tormenting the two younger members of the family. Elizabeth he rarely baited, as she was "a creature of some spirit," he claimed, and Sir Charles admired spirit . . . in women just as he did in horses.

As if in answer to Elizabeth's unspoken summons,

Lazenby walked in bearing a steaming silver teapot on a shining silver tray. The butler placed the tea ceremoniously on the table in front of her.

"Will that be all, Miss Elizabeth?"

Sir Charles broke in and dismissed him curtly before Elizabeth could reply. Lazenby crossed obediently but stiff-backed to the door, and the footman closed it quietly behind him.

Sir Charles immediately demanded coldly, "Why do the servants act as if I am not visible when you are present, Elizabeth?"

Elizabeth would have liked it infinitely better if his comment had really been a question instead of the accusation he had made it. She forced herself to answer smoothly, however.

"If I had to offer an explanation, I should say it is merely a habit, Sir Charles. After all, they had no one else to look to for their orders during the three years you were away from Chandering after Mother passed away."

Pain distorted his features. After a moment he mastered it and snarled, "Are you chiding me for my neglect of Chandering and of you two and the boy?"

"Of course not. You were coping with your grief at Mother's death, just as we were. No one can fault you for that." Her voice was soft and assured, and Sir Charles looked away, his hand clenching on the arm of his chair.

Elizabeth picked up a cup and added two lumps of sugar. After filling it with tea, she passed it to her sister and transferred her inquiring regard to Sir Charles.

"I shall have mine with cream today, if you please," Sir Charles said to Elizabeth, once more in control. He settled back in his chair. Then his gaze fell on Lucinda. He frowned slightly, as if puzzled.

"Your tea, Sir Charles." Elizabeth seemed to drag him out of a reverie by proffering the cup.

"Thank you," he said in a distracted manner.

Alerted by the odd quality of his voice, Elizabeth watched him as he turned his attention to the portrait of her mother that hung over the fireplace. It had been painted when the Viscountess was a bride. Lady Jessica Talbot Chanders. The young face smiled sweetly and radiantly from the heavy golden frame.

Elizabeth loved the portrait. She felt it had captured the quiet happiness that had been so much a part of her mother and of their lives.

She followed her stepfather's gaze as he turned it from the beautiful face on the canvas. For a moment his eyes rested on Lucinda, then he looked down thoughtfully at his cup as he stirred his tea.

Until now, Elizabeth had not noticed how much Lucinda looked like their beloved mother. Both had the golden hair and soft blue eyes of the Talbots, but now even the shape of Lucinda's face was becoming like that of her mother.

What a goose she was not to have noticed that her sister had become a beauty! Seeing her every day, she simply had not noticed when Lucinda had shed her adolescent plumpness and become a willowy vision.

She smiled fondly at Lucinda, who returned the smile, looking a little puzzled. Elizabeth mouthed "Later," and they turned their attention to Sir Charles as he spoke.

"I don't understand why you two were discussing adding flounces to old gowns. You are both fully aware that there is no necessity for such thrift. If it's a hint to me that you need clothes, it's a wasted effort. You know that I prefer directness in our relationship. If you need . . . indeed, if you merely wish for . . . new gowns, simply say so."

The sisters exchanged sheepish looks. The hasty excuse Lucinda had invented earlier had become an embarrassment. And they were trapped in it.

Elizabeth, always the spokesman, struggled a moment with her conscience, then said, "Perhaps a gown or two. We don't truly need them, but it would be nice to visit London to see what the newest styles and fabrics are."

"Oh, yes. Please!" Lucinda's face was alight. She loved new clothes and every last thing that went with them. So recently out of the schoolroom, fashion still occupied an important place in her world. She was all winsome supplication.

Elizabeth was all sympathy for her sister's enthusiasm. After all, while she had had most of a London Season, Lucinda had been a child in the schoolroom whose clothes were sent from London after an assistant had come out to Chandering to measure her.

She could well understand Lucinda's longing to be gowned by their mother's *modiste*, one of the best in London. And this was the first time a chance for a shopping trip had arisen in the four years since Jonathan's birth.

"Very well." Sir Charles's eyes warmed as they studied Lucinda's face. "I shall send you to town tomorrow."

Elizabeth watched Lucinda's delight with a small frown and wondered why she felt Sir Charles's offer had been made to Lucinda alone. She wondered, too, just what the sudden feeling of unease that had overtaken her could possibly mean.

Lifting the ornate silver teapot, and extending a graceful hand toward her stepfather, she made the only comment that came to her mind. "More tea?"

Chapter

* Four

Despite the excitement of a visit to Sir Charles's London town house, leaving Jonathan behind with the nursery staff was difficult for both sisters. Finally Bess, who, unlike their own Nanny Gray had been, could be quite formidable if the occasion demanded, whispered to Elizabeth her solemn word that she would see to his every comfort. All three of them knew this meant she would keep Jonathan out of his father's path. Only then did the two sisters allow themselves to be bundled into the waiting coach.

Sir Charles stood beside the well-sprung conveyance and smilingly admonished, "See that you order all that takes your fancy. I don't want either of you coming back here regretting some purchase you denied yourself."

He reached a hand toward his secretary and was handed a stout purse. "Thank you, Ponsonby. That will be all."

Ponsonby bowed himself away with a farewell smile for the two girls in the coach.

Suddenly Sir Charles stepped nearer and took Lucinda's hand from where it held the edge of the window. To the girl's surprise, he lifted it to his lips. An instant later he moved back and signaled the coachman to drive on.

"Well!" Lucinda could think of no more to say and sat, round-eyed, staring at Elizabeth.

"I don't believe he's ever done anything like that before," Elizabeth said musingly, her voice troubled.

"No, I should say not." Lucinda, already recovered from the surprise of her stepfather having kissed her hand, laughed.

"I had no idea he was so eager to be quit of us as all that!" Lucinda shrugged and put the incident out of her head with a toss of her curls. Her soft blue eyes twinkled roguishly at her sister's serious gray ones before she turned eagerly to wave goodbye to the gatekeeper's family.

Elizabeth only looked pensive as the horses began to gallop away the long miles to London.

"Ooo-la-la. Eet iz a happiness Mademoiselle has come to me. The dress she is becoming a little tight at Mademoiselle's bosoms, no?"

Elizabeth looked down at herself, startled. She fought a frown. The *modiste* was right, the fabric of her bodice was a trifle too snug. How annoying that she had not noticed that herself!

She knew she shouldn't resent the Frenchwoman's familiarity with *her* body, but it was one of those unreasoning things she couldn't help. She sighed, vexed with herself. Madame knew best. Of course she watched the figures of her clients like a hawk. It was her livelihood, after all, and the *ton* could be so cruelly fickle. It was greatly to Madame's credit that she had held sway over fashion for as long as she had.

Now that her straining bustline had been pointed out to her, Elizabeth was glad Sir Charles had sent them on this excursion. Just let one old tabby decide that Elizabeth intentionally wore her dresses too tight, and make that the subject of conversation, and the Honorable Elizabeth Chanders would be branded "fast." She scowled at the thought.

"Mademoiselle frowns! She is—*comment dit-on?* Piqued?"

"No, Madame. I merely frowned because I'm wondering what I shall wear home from your shop. As you say, it is a good thing I have come to you. I had not noticed my gain in . . . weight."

Indeed, Elizabeth thought how fortunate it was, also, that Lucinda's eagerness had brought them first to the *modiste*. Even stopping to choose a book to read during Lucinda's fitting could have resulted in social disaster had a dedicated gossip seen her dress!

That thought really made her want to frown. She sighed instead. How she disliked London society and its false standards! To turn a blind eye to an unfaithful wife's peccadillos, as long as she went about them discreetly, while censuring every false move made in ignorance by a green girl, struck her as hypocritical in the extreme.

She had no complaints about her own brief Season, though it had been cut short when her mother's "delicate condition" had become "difficult" and necessitated a return home. Elizabeth had taken it well and still corresponded with several of the friends she had made.

Their original plan had been to return to London at a later date, but her mother's condition had never improved. It had ended in her death at Jonathan's birth. No one had even thought of London again.

Until now.

Until Sir Charles had glanced at his late wife's portrait and then to her daughter's amazing resemblance . . .

Something akin to a premonition stirred uncomfortably in Elizabeth. "Absurd!" she pronounced heartily.

"Mademoiselle iz not pleased!" The *modiste* waved away the assistant holding a walking dress of soft gray wool. Her lips were pressed in a firm line.

Elizabeth could not apologize quickly enough. "Oh, no, Madame. The dress is lovely."

It was indeed just what she would like to wear back to the town house, though she would have accepted a burlap sack in order to smooth the ruffled feathers of the best *modiste* in London. Particularly since her own inexcusable loss of control had resulted in a *faux pas*.

"I was chiding myself for woolgathering. I didn't intend to speak aloud. Forgive me. The dress is lovely. Just exactly what I need to return home in without disgracing myself."

She turned her warmest smile on the little Frenchwoman. "How fortunate that you have something already made up that will, I am sure since you have chosen it, become me."

Madame was instantly all smiles. The assistant stepped forward again, and Elizabeth gave her full consideration to the matter at hand.

The late afternoon sun had further gilded Lucinda's blue and gold bedchamber by the time all the packages they had purchased had been opened. The bed was buried in a welter of gloves and slippers and fans and reticules and a dozen other items Lucinda needed to complete the outfits the *modiste* was preparing for her.

"Oooo, I can hardly wait!" Golden curls flying, she spun around, then ran to hug her sister. "Shall we not be slap up to the nines in all our new clothes?"

Elizabeth returned her hug and scolded, "A lady does not use vulgar speech."

Lucinda, neither offended nor contrite, laughed and said with a mock solemn stare, "Of course. I do beg pardon. I should have said that we shall look . . . top of the trees."

They fell into a fit of laughter then, both remembering the group of young men from whom they had overheard the cant Lucinda had used.

"Weren't they *impressed* with us, Elizabeth!"

"With you, dear. You are quite a beauty, you know."

"As are you, sister. I'm sure they were admiring us both as we strolled along Bond Street in magnificent dignity and pretended we never heard a word!"

"Well, it's quite obvious that you heard several, and I think that it would be a very good idea if you forgot them all."

Lucinda made a face, then whirled to the bed. "Do you think this blue will match the dress I bought it for?" She looked critically at a reticule, holding it toward Elizabeth.

"We can take it to Madame at our next fitting. If she doesn't think so, I'm sure she can have one made up that will."

"Hmmmm."

"What is it?"

"I'm just wondering what we shall do to fill the time while we wait to go home. No one is in town to speak of, and we don't know anybody, anyway."

Elizabeth smiled at her sister. "Then how do we know who is and isn't in town?"

Lucinda had the good grace to blush. "I've been reading Sir Charles's newspapers. They have a great deal of news about society in them."

"Sly puss. Does the *ton* interest you so much, then?"

"Oh, yes. Yes, it really does, Elizabeth. I find the news of the balls the most exciting, but all of their goings-on are of the greatest interest to me." She spoke eagerly, willing Elizabeth to understand and share her enthusiasm.

Elizabeth held back a sigh. She liked the city well enough, but she would never be able to match Lucinda's eagerness. She truly preferred the country, spiced, perhaps, with an occasional foray into town to see a play or attend a ball that held special meaning for a friend. But the exhausting whirl of balls, soirees, and parties that constituted a London Season left her singularly unmoved.

What could she do for Lucinda? She could speak to Sir Charles. Lucinda was seventeen, certainly of an age to make her come-out, and no mention of any plans had been made.

She sighed. For the thousandth time she wished that Sir Charles had asked one of the older women in the family to reside with them. Someone wise in the things necessary to ready a young girl for her come-out.

There was nothing for it, she mused, falling into the very trap of using cant that she had chided her sister for. On their return to Chandering she must speak to Sir Charles about bringing Lucinda out this Season.

Lucinda's eighteenth birthday was in April, so no one could think her too young, certainly. Yes, she must most definitely speak to Sir Charles.

But why did she feel a little trepidation at the thought of doing so? Surely things were not so unpleasant between them that she could not remind him of his duty to Lucinda's future?

She gave herself a mental shake. No wonder she

preferred country life if London was the cause of the strange starts she'd been having lately.

Lucinda grabbed her hands and pulled her toward the door. "Go and dress for dinner, my inattentive, solemn sister. Even if they were not made specifically for me, I'm still excited at the thought of wearing a new dress. Go. Find an especially pretty one and look your best for our first evening in London!"

Elizabeth smiled at her sister's enthusiasm and hurried to her room. She must take great pains tonight. It would never do to dim her dear Lucinda's happiness at being here in town.

She tried to shake off all her dismal forebodings . . . brought on, no doubt, by having to leave her beloved Socrates at home! She refused even to think of Jonathan—except to vow to find him the finest presents available in all London—instead, she promised herself that she would think of ways to show Lucinda the great city.

She pledged herself to making their brief stay in London a joyous one for her sister, then rang for her maid. The first part of keeping that promise was before her. Lucinda had set Elizabeth no less a task than to decide how to look positively dazzling while having a perfectly quiet, albeit very elegant, of course, dinner at home.

CHAPTER
✳ FIVE

"It's indeed a handsome property, Marc, though why the devil you had to drag us five miles out of our way to look at it is completely beyond me," Anthony, Lord Stayne, complained.

"Because, you young jackanapes, Chandering is yours when the younger sister attains the age of twenty-one . . . or marries. I thought it high time you took a look at it." The man on the big bay grimaced as he shifted his left leg, easing it from the stirrup to hang stiffly down his horse's side.

His brother leaned closer to search his face, taking care that none of the worry he felt showed on his own handsome one, and that his voice was suitably disinterested. "Hmmm. I think we will spend a day or two at the nearest inn. You look pretty well done up, and I'd wager a monkey that leg could use a little time out of the saddle. And God knows I, for one, don't want to live with reproachful looks from your staff at Castle Wynmalen for the remainder of my stay there."

"We're for Castle Wynmalen, Tony. I'll sleep in my own bed tonight, thank you! And furthermore . . ." Marcus Stayne, Earl of Wynmalen, told his brother exactly what he thought of his unsolicited concern in words any soldier would readily understand.

"Very well." Unruffled, Tony Stayne drawled,

"We'll ride for Castle Wynmalen, then. But I hope"—
his eyebrow lifted quizzically and he touched his crop
to the back of his hat, tilting it even farther over his
eyes—"that you'll be so kind as to let me know if you
would care to break our journey at any point." He
cantered off, whistling, leaving Wynmalen to follow.

Wynmalen swore softly under his breath as he
attempted to place his foot back in its stirrup. He held
his impatiently dancing stallion in check more by his
iron will than by his hand on the reins. Finally the stiff
leg obeyed, and the boot slipped onto the stirrup bar.

He'd make it to his ancestral seat and sleep in his
own bed tonight if it killed him! To that end, he gave
his huge bay stallion its head and thundered in
pursuit, his sleek black mastiff running easily behind.

A scant mile away the younger sister of their brief
conversation was saying breathlessly, "Astley's was
wonderful, Jonathan. I hope you shall be able to see it
soon! London is a great bustling city. Quite over-
whelming at first, I promise you!" Lucinda glowed
with enthusiasm, and her little half brother stared
with eyes round in fascination.

Sir Charles was even content to let Jonathan stay in
the room as he himself watched his vivacious step-
daughter with obvious pleasure. At one point he
laughed aloud, and Elizabeth was startled to hear him
say, "By Gad, I'm glad I didn't deliver you to your
guardian after all."

As she puzzled over his peculiar comment, Elizabeth wondered why she must always be at variance
with the mood in a room. In London she had been
suspicious of Sir Charles's sudden generosity. Now
she was mistrustful of his geniality. She sighed, thoroughly irritated with herself.

With an effort, she forced herself to smile and at least seem to enjoy Lucinda's prattle. Now where did that word come from? she wondered. She would enjoy her sister's delight in her trip to London. Prattle, indeed!

Was she, sensible Elizabeth, becoming a hateful old maid? Surely not. Not if she could help it, at any rate. And now that she had caught herself being mentally uncharitable, she'd accept wagers that she wouldn't let it happen again!

". . . and Elizabeth knows just where to go. She is the best guide imaginable."

"Perhaps, my dear." Sir Charles's voice was warm and intimate. "But there are other entertainments. Entertainments of a more . . . interesting nature that a young lady alone could not possibly have shown you."

Elizabeth's gaze snapped to his face. The words had almost been a caress. She was shocked to find his eyes hot with . . . with what? She struggled to put a name to what she saw on her stepfather's face. Try as she would to avoid it, she could only call it . . .

Her stomach tightened, and the teacup clattered against its saucer in her hand. Ice seemed to encase her very being. This must not be!

As if from far away, she saw her dear, innocent Lucinda laughingly recounting their stroll down Bond Street on the day they had encountered the young dandies from whom Lucinda had learned the cant she now shared with her brother. And she saw her stepfather's nostrils flare like those of a hound on the scent.

Her mind shied away from her speculations. She could not bear to think such things! Obviously she was overtired and needed rest. Lucinda needed rest, too. It had been a long day, coming home to Chandering. Surely her tired mind was betraying her. *Surely* it was that and nothing more.

Nevertheless, her hand shook as she replaced her cup and saucer on the tea tray with a clink. She rose abruptly. "Jonathan, it is well past your bedtime. Please go up at once." Her voice, not quite steady, sounded strange to her own ears.

Lucinda stared at her, surprised and a little hurt by the interruption.

Elizabeth felt as if her nerves were approaching some breaking point . . . as if she most urgently had to get her sister away, safe from the avid eyes of her stepfather. "I have a most dreadful headache," she lied. "Please forgive my abruptness." She passed her trembling hand across her brow. "Luce, would you help me to bed? I don't know when I have felt so peculiar."

That at least was true. She felt trapped in a morass of horrid suspicions. She prayed desperately that a good night's sleep would drive away her warped fancies and take away the awful feeling that she was going to cry at any moment.

Lucinda moved immediately to her side. "Dearest, you are quite pale. I should've noticed and not run on so." Deeply solicitous, Lucinda touched a shapely hand to her sister's forehead.

"Pray hold us excused, Sir Charles," Lucinda said firmly, taking charge of the situation. Slipping an arm around Elizabeth, she led her from the room without a backward glance.

In response to a warning shout from one of his ostlers, the innkeeper rushed out onto his porch just in time to see two men ride into the yard of his establishment.

The younger gentleman was supporting the other, who seemed to be half-conscious. He called to the innkeeper, "Your two finest bedchambers, my man. And come help me get my brother down."

As the innkeeper hurried down the steps, Tony Stayne warned him. "Quietly! I'd hate to see his dog tear an arm off you."

"Aye, milord." The stout little man stopped a moment to let the wary dog calm down, then walked slowly and deliberately toward the horses, gesturing for the ostler to help him remove the half-swooning gentleman from his saddle. The big stallion watched them, eyes rolling.

Ignoring the low growls from the throat of the black mastiff, Tony Stayne and the innkeeper helped Wynmalen up the two broad steps into the ordinary as the ostler led their horses away to be rubbed down and bedded deep.

Half an hour later the two gentlemen were settled in the best bedchambers. The Earl was firmly tucked up in spite of feeble protests even the village idiot would have recognized as merely token resistance.

After Tony Stayne had seen to his brother's comfort, he opened the door into the cozy sitting room situated between Marcus's room and his own.

The huge black dog stretched out on the rug beside Wynmalen's bed followed the youth's movements with his eyes. His tail thumped once in acknowledgment of Tony's "Good boy, Valiant. Guard." Then he lowered his head to his paws as Stayne closed the door quietly behind him.

When the younger gentleman called for a bottle of the best brandy, the innkeeper decided that any man who rode such a fine horse must have a purse as plump as one could wish, and the brandy . . . good

French brandy . . . was brought from where the inn kept it hidden from less worthy eyes. The staff of the Boar and Castle was nothing if not efficient in seeing to the needs of the Quality.

Less than an hour later, Wynmalen, worn out with the pain that was now deadened by the half a bottle of brandy his brother had forced down him, slept at last.

Tony, bone weary after the better part of two days in the saddle and mentally exhausted by the constant strain of watching his brother tax himself beyond his strength, tossed for hours.

Long he pondered the problem of just what he could do to keep Marcus from riding himself into the ground before he was fully recovered from the wounds he'd received on the Continent. Finally, blessedly, sleep claimed him.

In the darkest hour of the night, Elizabeth was roused from the deep sleep into which her fit of weeping had pitched her. She sat up in bed, the silence of the great house all around her, knowing something was dreadfully amiss.

What could have disturbed her? She stilled her breathing to listen, a hand at her throat. Nothing. No stealthy footsteps. No voices. What in the world was the matter with her?

Disgusted by this further display of nerves, she flopped back on her pillows. Punching her fist into one of them, she turned on her side and made a determined effort to empty her mind.

She sighed. It was no use. Something nagged at her, denying her peace. Finally, with a sigh of aggravation that shook her whole frame, she bounced to the side of her wide bed, slid off its edge, and reached for her wrapper as she fumbled her feet into her slippers.

She would just go stand at the top of the stairs and listen. Then she would be assured that there was nothing wrong. The great house was not on fire. Jonathan was not hanging from a window ledge, howling. There were no robbers running through the halls. She was simply being foolish.

In her mind she was certain of all these things, but still she needed to stand quietly at the top of the grand staircase, a spot to which every sound in Chandering carried, and assure her restless mind that all was well. Otherwise she knew she would toss and turn the rest of the night.

Crossing the familiar room in total darkness, she arrived at the door a little sooner than she expected, and her outstretched hand hit the panel solidly.

"Ouch," she muttered, twisting the door handle a little harder than was necessary. She pulled the tall door inward and stepped confidently through the doorway.

Once in the hall, she could see her way by the candles left burning at intervals in the hallway sconces. She started toward the grand stairwell, her slippered feet noiseless on the smooth parquet.

"I'm probably just overtired from traveling," she grumbled.

The tall clock in the hall outside the library struck the hour. Three o'clock! She was beginning to feel exceedingly silly parading through the house in the dead of night.

Suddenly her heart was in her throat. Surely she had heard a sound in the very hall in which she walked. Slowing her steps, holding her breath, she crept forward.

Just ahead, in a shadowy part of the hall, she heard footsteps! Quickly she flattened herself against the wall, thankful that the deep blue of her wrapper would make her invisible in the dimness, praying that the swish of her skirts hadn't given her away.

Whoever could be walking the halls at *this* hour? Carefully craning her neck, she looked around the statue behind which she hid.

Sir Charles! It was Sir Charles, and he reached, even as she watched, eyes wide with shock, for the handle of the door before which he stood. For the handle of the door to Lucinda's bedchamber!

CHAPTER
❋ SIX

Elizabeth knew that at all costs, she must act as if everything were perfectly normal this morning. If she betrayed her true feelings by even the smallest hint, she would never be able to extract from her stepfather the information that she *must* have!

In a gesture totally foreign to her usually calm nature, she wiped her hands nervously down the sides of her skirts as she approached the door to the east drawing room. She schooled her features into a bland expression and, as the footman opened the door, walked casually into the room.

Lucinda was there, lovely in her pale muslin morning dress. She rose immediately to greet her. "Dearest, I hope you are feeling more the thing this morning." Concern filled her countenance.

"Yes, thank you. And thank you, too, for sending me my tray this morning. Breakfast in my bed was a wonderful treat." She brushed a kiss on Lucinda's cheek and acknowledged Sir Charles's curt greeting with a nod.

On arising this morning she'd told Lucinda to support her in the lie she'd told him about wanting a headache powder. That had been the excuse she'd used to take her past her stepfather and into her sister's room in the wee hours of this morning.

Elizabeth had not, however, awakened Lucinda, and had certainly not told her that their stepfather, smelling decidedly of brandy, had been about to enter her room. Nor had she shared with her younger sister her fears for her person.

She knew she was right to keep her own horrors from Lucinda. The girl was not used to dissembling, and Elizabeth *must* keep her suspicions from Sir Charles until her plans to remove her precious sister from his contaminating presence were in place.

Even now, in the pleasant light of day, Elizabeth had to be careful to control herself lest she give way to her body's desire to shudder every time she thought of the intention on Sir Charles's face as he stood before her sleeping sister's door.

"I trust you are recovered, Elizabeth." Sir Charles's voice failed to betray the slightest trace of concern for Elizabeth's illness. "I waited some time outside Lucinda's door and was troubled when you did not return."

Elizabeth thought she could feel her sister's slight start. Was she shocked to learn that her stepfather had been prowling near her room? Or could Lucinda have been somehow aware of Sir Charles in the dark beyond her door? And most importantly, was she fearful because of it?

Elizabeth dared not look at her to see. "I fear I fell asleep as Lucinda stroked my brow to ease the headache."

Not daring to permit Lucinda to say that her own sleep had been undisturbed, Elizabeth hurried to say, "Shall I help you finish sorting your threads, dearest?" She simply must have something to occupy her hands—some excuse not to look into her stepfather's eyes.

"Would you? How nice. I'll get my embroidery

basket before you change your mind." Lucinda suited action to words and crossed the room to retrieve her embroidery from the window seat.

Sir Charles looked up from the letters he had been skimming to watch her graceful form as Lucinda walked to the window and returned.

Elizabeth tried not to notice the avid look on his face. Then he slowly moistened his lips, and she blurted out, "Sir Charles. Last evening you said that you were glad you had not sent us to our guardian. I was not aware we had a guardian. You've raised in me an insatiable curiosity." She hoped her smile was inquiring and not sick, as she felt it must be.

"Oh!" Lucinda's blue eyes were full of curiosity. "Do please tell us why in the world we would have a guardian when we had you and . . ." She couldn't add "Mother." Even after four years the pain of missing her was too great.

"You have no guardian," Sir Charles snapped. "Such a thing would be absurd when you have me to look after you and your interests."

"But you did say . . ." Lucinda was obviously not going to drop so intriguing a subject.

Sir Charles looked into her eyes, so like his beloved late wife's, and was powerless to deny her the information he would gladly have kept from Elizabeth, if only for spite.

He sighed in exasperation, then said, "Your father and mother had asked a young officer on your father's staff, a distant cousin I believe, to stand *in loco parentis*—in place of your parents—if anything should befall them at the time of your mother's visit to him on the Continent. The battle, you see, was not so far removed from where the Colonel was quartered that he felt your mother entirely safe, I imagine." A black scowl formed on his face. "I have never understood how he could endanger her so."

Elizabeth, smarting slightly at his assumption that it was necessary to explain to them one of the most common of Latin phrases, was now further stung by the slur on her father. She couldn't resist saying, "They were so very much in love. Nothing could have kept Mama from his side."

Seeing the pain flash across his face, she was almost sorry she had spoken. She bit her lip and reached for a handful of tangled silks from her sister's basket.

"But who was it?" Lucinda insisted. "Mama never so much as mentioned a guardian."

"He was only a young officer then. He has inherited since, and the former Lieutenant Marcus Stayne is now the Earl of Wynmalen, if you must know. Now that you are beyond the need of his care, I'm doubtful if he even has any recollection of his duty to you. I'd almost forgotten myself." He returned his attention dismissively to his correspondence, his expression sour.

Elizabeth wanted to shout in triumph. She had the name of the friend to whom her parents would have entrusted Lucinda and her! Surely if he'd been willing to look after the interests of a pair of girl children, he was the sort of man she could turn to for the rescue and safekeeping of her dear Lucinda.

With her head dutifully bent over the snarl Lucinda had made of her embroidery threads, Elizabeth began to make her plans.

The sun streamed into the private parlor shared by the Staynes, covering the floor with diamond-patterned golden light. The fire on the hearth added its warmth to the room, and the aroma of the hearty

breakfast Tony had ordered spoke beguilingly to yet
another of their senses.

Wynmalen sat at ease in a wing chair beside the
fireplace, his injured leg stretched out before him on a
stool stacked with cushions. On his lap, tenderly
guarded by his left hand, rested a small stack of
much-read letters. His right hand held one as if he
read it, but he had no need of the fragile paper, for he
had long ago committed the words thereon to fondest
memory.

Tony watched his brother's face carefully. Still lined
with the pain their journey had caused his war
wounds, it was nevertheless more relaxed than it had
been in the months since his return from the army.

Tony hoped he could induce Marcus to remain here
at the inn at least another two days. Being away from
the cares imposed by the management of his huge
estate was doing Marcus a world of good. His bailiff
was an excellent man, and Marcus could well afford to
be absent. If only he could make Marcus realize it.

"Emily's letters?" he inquired softly.

"Yes." Marc's smile lit his face. "What a lucky dog
I am, Tony. She's an angel to have stuck by me."

"A sensible decision. You're more man injured than
most of the men whole in London." He didn't add,
one of the richest, too.

He had to admit that he was pleased and grateful
that Lady Emily Simms had not thrown Marc over
when he came home wounded beyond restoration to
his former grace.

Even taking into account Marc's wealth, it had
seemed to Tony out of character for Emily to hold to
her betrothal to a disfigured man. Hell, his brother
was all the more interesting to his male companions
with the scar on his face, but members of the fairer sex

were often put off by it, and he was glad, and more than a little surprised, to find that Emily was apparently made of sterner stuff.

Betraying no hint of his thoughts, he said, "I would like to stay here another day or two, Marc. To rest. The next time you get a notion to check on your bailiff at Wyndhaven, pray forget to invite me. You've worn me out with your mad tear around the countryside."

Marcus's head snapped up. "I'm certain you don't expect me to believe such rot." Wynmalen's tone was sharp. He knew it was unreasonable in him, but he couldn't help resenting attempts to coddle him. There had been no invitation to Tony. Tony had forced his company on Wynmalen out of concern, and Wynmalen knew it.

"Well, actually there is a comely little dairy maid . . ."

"Oh, for God's sake, Tony! Another of your irresistible treats, no doubt."

"Sowing the old wild oats, you know, Marc. You've thrown me into a panic by threatening to see me leg-shackled as soon as you find someone you can bully into serving as my jailor."

"Would that I but knew her name, I'd find her if I had to search the whole of England!"

Tony, smiling at his brother's empty threat, cajoled, "Just one more day, Marc. Surely you can grant me just one more day?"

For a moment Marcus, thinking of the many duties that awaited him, scowled. Then his face, almost reluctantly, relaxed and he nodded.

Tony's grin was wide. His deception had won his brother another day of much needed rest. Now all he had to do was find a milkmaid. . . .

Chapter

❊ Seven

Gone! Finally he was gone. Now she could set about implementing her plans for their escape. No! First she must be certain!

Elizabeth ran to the window in a flurry of skirts and peered out into the late afternoon. Yes, Sir Charles's chaise was almost at the gatehouse. He was truly on his way to Squire Baxter's!

Lucinda, startled by the sudden change in her sister's demeanor, asked, "What in the world has come over you, Elizabeth? What is of such great interest that you rush so to see it?"

"Our stepfather's departure," Elizabeth said cryptically, and hurried back to her sister's side. "Lucinda, you must trust me. Can I count on you to do so?"

"You silly goose. You know I would trust you with my life. Why, however, do you suddenly look like a character from a Cheltenham tragedy?" She studied her sister's face with concern. "Are you all right, dearest?"

"Oh, I'm as fine as I can be in the circumstances. But we've no time to discuss that. Listen. I've had Henson smuggle a trunk to your room. Please go and, as swiftly as you can, choose sensible clothing for a week or two away from home."

Elizabeth ignored Lucinda's attempt to question

her. Better to explain later when they were safely
away. "Hurry, dearest. It's already so late!" she insisted, propelling an agog Lucinda toward the staircase. "I'll bring my things to your room, so leave me a
little space in the trunk, if you please. We've only the
one."

At the top of the stairs, Lucinda protested breathlessly, "But Elizabeth . . ." She spoke to thin air. Her
sister was already halfway down the hall to her own
bedchamber.

"Elizabeth, I simply cannot imagine what you think
you are about! I *must* demand an explanation. Now!"
Lucinda stood stubbornly rooted to the gravel in the
drive, staring incredulously at the figure of her sister.

"Lucinda, you promised to trust me, and there isn't
time now. Get in the coach!"

Beautiful Lucinda did the impossible and looked
like a mule.

"Where are we goin', 'Lizbeth?" Jonathan's voice
was full of excitement.

"Later, Jonathan. You, too, will have to trust me for
a little while. We must get as much distance between
us and Chandering as may be managed before Sir
Charles returns."

"Oooo!" Jonathan exclaimed, his eyes big with
wonder. "We are running away from home, aren't we,
'Lizbeth?"

Elizabeth stilled her mad urge for haste to answer
her little half brother. "Yes, my angel, we are. Do you
mind awfully? We can't take Pony."

Jonathan considered her words gravely. "I suppose
that will be all right. After all, I am getting bigger, and
Pony is getting very old, Jack says."

"Yes, darling." She stopped to kiss his cheek. "Now please get in."

Jonathan climbed obediently into the traveling coach, and Elizabeth turned to Lucinda. "Well? Are you going to trust me until I can get you away, or are you going to stand there staring at me like a pea-goose?"

Lucinda gave a very unladylike snort. "I suppose you would take it quite in stride and not even *blink* at me if I were standing here dressed in that outfit?"

Elizabeth heaved a sigh of exasperation. "I will satisfy your curiosity when we arrive at Castle Wynmalen. Until then, I hope you won't find it too taxing to keep your promise to trust me." She glanced at her sister.

"Very well." Lucinda glared back. "I keep my promises." With that she flounced into the conveyance and flopped down beside Jonathan, rocking the coach on its springs. "You'd better have a good reason for appearing abroad garbed as a gentleman. And I'd better hear it soon!" With that she slammed the window shut.

Elizabeth swung up into her saddle with ease. Not for the first time, she envied men their fashions.

"Steady, Soc," she calmed Socrates. The big gelding had become fractious at the unaccustomed anger in the voices of the two sisters.

Elizabeth chuckled. She found that she was less moved than the sensitive Thoroughbred. She knew Lucinda would be herself by the time they stopped at the first inn. Elizabeth never worried when they had a tiff. She knew Lucinda's sweet nature would quickly reassert itself.

She settled comfortably in the saddle. From her labors in the library most of the morning, Elizabeth knew that the inn she sought was a good fifteen miles away, and at the pace she set, could easily be gained in under two hours.

There she'd hire a post chaise to take them on the rest of their journey. There she could become herself again as well. She hoped the need to throw their stepfather off their trail by appearing to be a young couple, rather than two young ladies, should be past by then.

Fortunately, Elizabeth's big chestnut was just that, a big chestnut, with no distinguishing marks to make him memorable. He could be tied to the back of the post chaise and taken to Wynmalen with them safely, so long as the man's saddle she was riding was left behind, hidden somewhere.

The day was passing swiftly. The shadows were already long and the evening beginning to cool.

Well, there was nothing to be done about the lateness of the hour, except to be grateful that the moon promised to be bright and push on. There had been no way to get away any earlier.

While she was feeling appreciative of the bright night, she must also be grateful for Henson and Lazenby, who had helped get them away. For Bess, too, who even now sat with her back to the horses and Jonathan under her watchful eye. No one was taking her dear little fledgling without taking her as well! And last, but, oh, certainly not least, for Tom Coachman. Without him they would surely have failed in their endeavor, because, even though she was very good at driving her tilbury, Elizabeth could never have driven the coach with its four perfectly matched—and perfectly mettlesome—grays.

She flashed a glance at the stolid man on the box—whose name was actually John Allworthy. He caught the movement of her head and smiled—a grim, brief smile—down at her.

She was relieved she had thought of hiring a post chaise at the inn to continue their journey. With a sufficient bribe the innkeeper would, no doubt, conveniently forget their destination. But, more important, John Allworthy would be safely back at Chandering before her stepfather had played his last hand of cards at Squire Baxter's.

Even if later Sir Charles were to question John about their disappearance, she was certain he would never give them away. He had been Father's coachman, after all.

As the miles rolled under them, she found herself hoping she'd done all she should. She knew the futility of going over plans that had already been put in motion, but she couldn't help herself.

Her cheeks flamed momentarily as she remembered the shock of Ponsonby's grave face when she had coolly appropriated the household money and left the startled secretary holding her promissory note to repay at a later date.

He had made no move to stop her, though. Nor had he questioned her weak excuse that Great Aunt Agatha had suddenly been taken ill.

In fact, she thought she had detected an understanding light in his eyes as he had stood in the doorway at Lazenby's side and quietly wished them Godspeed.

Servants always knew all that went on beneath the roof of their great house. Could it be that she was not the only one to feel it was necessary to distance Lucinda from Sir Charles?

On that sober thought, Elizabeth drew her cloak closer and set her face firmly in the direction of the estate known to her only as Castle Wynmalen.

God grant that the man who had so long ago served
with her father would remember his promise to his
Colonel to guard his daughters. Of course, his agreement had been made to be guardian to a pair of
schoolgirls. She hoped she could convince her father's
young officer to stretch his long ago obligation to
allow him, now, to take on two young ladies and their
little half brother.

God grant her the ability to make him understand
their need to flee their home. What a tangle! With
every mile her heart grew fainter. What had looked so
simple under her desperation to protect her sister now
seemed less than easy to explain to an unknown,
long-hoped-for benefactor.

She could only fervently pray that the man known
now as Wynmalen would give them sanctuary.

The inn yard was a picture of confusion when
Elizabeth rode into it. The ostlers were busy with
another traveling coach, a heavy, mud-splattered
thing pulled by four poorly matched horses. She
swung down from Socrates to tell Lucinda and Bess
that it would be a few minutes before they could leave
their coach.

The burly man in the vehicle ahead of them seemed
intent on being as troublesome to the stablemen as he
could manage. He showed no inclination to hurry his
business so that the second coach might be accommo-
dated sooner.

Thinking to spend profitably the time she was being
forced to wait, Elizabeth told Socrates, "Stay," as if he
were some huge dog, and the gelding dropped his
head and stood, hip-shot, resting until the ostlers had
time to tend him.

Elizabeth picked her way through the steaming

evidence of horse traffic that dotted the cobbled yard
at intervals and started up the steps to the inn porch.

Entering the bright warmth of the inn, she hesitated
just inside the door, drawing off her gauntlets. Glanc-
ing about, she saw two tall men, one blond and one
dark, entering a private parlor, and a small crowd of
farmers taking their ease in the public room.

The innkeeper had just noticed her in the doorway
and started over to Elizabeth when a rough hand
dropped on her shoulder.

Spinning her around to face him, the heavyset man
from the inn yard yelled into her face, "So, stripling,
you think to push yourself ahead of me, do you?"

Elizabeth, appalled by the man's manners, answered firmly, "There is no need to shout, sir."

"No need to shout! Would you teach me my
manners then, young puppy?"

Elizabeth was in a quandary. Without an older
brother, she was rather at a loss to imagine just what
response might be expected of her. Surely no young
gentleman would tolerate such treatment, but what in
the world would he do about it? Especially in the face
of such overwhelming odds! The man made three of
her.

Certainly a young gentleman would not countenance the familiarity of a stranger's hand on his
person! Very well. "Please be so good as to remove
your hand from my person." There—that sounded
about right.

The man was speechless with rage.

What a bother. She had no sword, no stick, no
pocket pistol. And she *certainly* had no skill at fisticuffs. Heavens, what was she expected to do about
this very rude and intrusive man?

Suddenly the matter was taken out of her hands.

With purposeful stride, one of the men she had seen enter the private parlor approached. Elizabeth had just time to notice that he was the dark one and that, in spite of a scar on his left cheek, he was extremely handsome.

He tapped the bully on the shoulder. "Sir, I beg leave to tell you that the loudness of your comments is disturbing my dinner," he drawled.

"Plague take you and your dinner. I've this whelp to take care of." With that the man turned again to Elizabeth and, raising his arm, slammed a fist straight into her jaw.

If the man with the scar on his face had not caught at his arm as he swung, Elizabeth's delicate jaw would have shattered, she had no doubt.

As it was, her head flew back and hit the wall behind her with a crack. Uttering a faint and very feminine "Oooh," she found herself sliding weakly down the wall to land in a heap at its foot.

The man who had attempted to stop the blow let out a mighty curse and bent quickly to aid her, his blue eyes flaming.

"Oh, no, you don't, scarface! I'll not have you interfering with the lesson I'm teaching."

The scarred man straightened with Elizabeth's unconscious body in his arms and snarled, "You damned fool. See what you've done!"

He attempted to shoulder his way past the man with his burden, intent on getting what he now had no doubt was a young woman to the privacy of the parlor he had just left.

"Not so fast!" The bully threw out an arm blocking Wynmalen's path.

Fury suffused the Earl's face. The force of anger in his eyes bore the other man back a step. Then, in a voice that had moved men on a battlefield, he roared, "Valiant! To me."

With a scramble of heavy claws and the thud of his huge body careening off a wall, the Earl of Wynmalen's black mastiff, fangs bared, arrived on the scene.

"Attack!" Wynmalen set the beast on the man, little caring whether he merely held or killed the boor.

Valiant launched himself from powerful haunches, and the bully went down with a shriek of terror. The dog's slavering jaws were inches from the man's throat as he slammed to his back on the floor of the hall.

"God's mercy! Call off your dog!"

With one withering glance of scorn, the dog's master spat, "Move and he'll tear your throat out!"

With that less than reassuring word to the prostrate tyrant, he kicked open the door to his private parlor and, bearing Elizabeth within, laid her on the settee before the fire.

"What in God's name . . . ?" Tony leapt from his chair and moved to his brother's side.

Flinging his after-dinner cigar into the fireplace, he peered at Elizabeth an instant. "A woman by all that's holy! What the devil is she doing in a rig like that?" He looked with disapproval at the outmoded clothes of some young gentleman that covered the girl's slender figure.

At that instant, his eyes rolling nervously, the innkeeper knocked on the jamb of the open door, cleared his throat, and opened his mouth to speak.

"Why are you standing there? Bring cold water and brandy, and be quick about it," Wynmalen snapped. He was too used to being instantly obeyed to even glance at the little man.

The innkeeper, a self-taught student of humanity, stopped twisting his hands behind his apron and lost no time. Nervously skirting the fallen Squire Larkin and the dog on his chest, he was off to the kitchen for a bowl of water before the deep reverberations of Wynmalen's commanding voice had died.

Squire Larkin's desperate pleas for help went unheeded by the innkeeper on his return trip as well. Not for anything would he brave the wrath of the huge, snarling mastiff. Nor, for that matter, of his equally formidable master.

CHAPTER
✳ EIGHT

Lucinda pushed away Bess's restraining hand and reached for the handle of the coach door. "I'm going to see what has happened to Elizabeth. She has been gone far too long now, Bess."

"We'll come with you, Miss Lucinda. It's not fitting that you should enter an inn unattended. Just wait till I wake the young one." Bess bent over Jonathan, speaking to him softly.

Lucinda tripped the latch and jumped lightly down onto the cobblestones. Gathering her pale muslin skirts close about her, she crossed to the inn door. She had the most dreadful feeling that something had happened to Elizabeth!

The first sight to greet her did nothing to allay her fears. The prostrate body of a man lay on the floor just inside the doorway—Squire Larkin, if the voices calling out unnecessary advice to lie still were to be trusted.

As she hesitated in the doorway, her wide blue eyes fastened on the slavering dog, she heard a man in the rough clothes of a farmhand speak.

"Serves 'im right, I sez. 'E'd no cause to maul down the poor lad like 'e did."

"Aye," a second countryman agreed. "Let 'im lay, sez I."

With a general murmur of agreement the men who had been filling the hall moved back to their pints in the common room, leaving the way clear for an agitated Lucinda to rush by in search of her sister.

There was no doubt in her mind that the lad who had been "mauled down" was her precious Elizabeth. She must find her immediately!

"Landlord!" she cried as the man hurried into view followed by a maid carrying a pitcher and a bowl. The innkeeper stopped so abruptly the brandy in the decanter he bore slopped against its stopper.

"Where is my . . . brother?"

The innkeeper goggled at the young lady. A real diamond of the first water, a sight he was rarely privileged to see in his quiet inn. Finally he managed, "Here, milady. Where we be going." He nodded at the door of a private parlor.

Lucinda threw herself at it before he could reach the door to open it for her, and burst into the room to see two tall men bending over Elizabeth's still form.

In a flash she was at her sister's side. Catching a limp hand to her cheek she cried, "Oh, dearest. Do speak to me." She lifted tear-misted eyes to the young gentleman beside her sister. "Pray, sir, is she all right?"

Tony, struck dumb, only stared at the dainty apparition.

Wynmalen was in better case and assured her, "She'll soon be right as a trivet. The blow was a light one. She'll be around in a moment."

He held a cold cloth to the half-conscious girl's jaw and told his brother drily, "If you would like to help matters, Tony, I think a spot of brandy might do the trick."

Tony tore his gaze away from Lucinda and held a

glass with a few spoonfuls of brandy in it to the other
girl's lips.

Elizabeth swallowed, sputtered as the brandy
burned its way down her throat, and opened wide
gray eyes. Dazedly she looked straight into the vivid
blue ones of the man with the scarred face.

She was weakly struggling to rise, eyes still a little
unfocused, when a whirlwind burst into the room and
threw itself against the legs of the tall blond who had
given her the brandy.

"Don't you dare hurt my sister! You leave my
'Lizbeth alone!" Jonathan manfully pummeled his foe,
until Tony, by the simple expedient of a hand rested in
Jonathan's golden curls, held him at bay.

Bess puffed into the room and enfolded the raging
child in her arms, "Forgive him, sir, he's overset." She
stroked Jonathan's hair. "There, there, my love. Bess
has you. All's well, all's well."

Jonathan threw both arms around his ample nursemaid and glared at Tony from under his curls.

Tony smiled at the boy reassuringly, but won no
smile in answer. Determined to put the truculent child
at ease, the man bowed seriously to the boy. "It is I
who must ask your forgiveness, sir," he said gravely.
"I assure you we wish your sister no harm."

There was a brief hesitation, then Jonathan stood
forth out of the shelter of his nursemaid's arms.
Bowing in imitation of the golden Adonis before him,
he said with great dignity and a condescending nod,
"You are forgibben, sir."

Tony looked quickly away to hide his smile and met
the approving regard of the lovely blond who had
rushed to her stricken sister's aid. For a moment their
glances held, then she turned away in pretty confusion.

A sudden warmth of emotion coursed through him. Tony looked startled.

Elizabeth, sitting upright with the support of Wynmalen's arm around her shoulders, passed an uncertain hand across her eyes. Still earnestly studying his face, she murmured, "Heavens. Why ever do men go to boxing establishments? I declare *I* can perceive no enjoyment to be had in this art of fisticuffs."

The dark-haired man with the scar smiled—a slash of strong white teeth in his tanned face. Elizabeth stared at him bemusedly. He was very nice to look at. Such character and strength in that face.

Wynmalen saw gray eyes, as clear as morning mist, as honest as a babe's. They perused his face in a languid fashion, seeming to study it.

He felt himself tense as those eyes ran lightly over his disfigured cheek, made nothing of it, and passed on. A feeling he couldn't quite define stirred in him. Was it relief?

The young lady, not yet herself, studied at length the firm sculpture of his lips, causing him to take a sudden deep breath.

As his nostrils flared, Elizabeth came to herself. "Oh, dear. I was staring. How dreadfully rude. Please forgive me."

"Nonsense," Wynmalen said bracingly, wondering why he felt in need of yet another deep breath. "You've been unconscious."

"Yes, and I believe I have you to thank that it was not a great deal worse." The gray eyes met his openly. "Only think what might have happened if you hadn't caught his arm!" She pressed a slender hand to the tender spot on her jaw.

Wynmalen felt a flash of savage fury at the thought of the damage the half-drunk bully could have done this gallant young lady if he'd not chanced to interfere. He listened with intense satisfaction to the attempts the man in question was making to placate the slavering Valiant.

As if she were aware of the direction of his thoughts, Lucinda looked at him in admiration. "Is, then, the large dog in the hallway yours, sir?"

"Yes, his name is Valiant. I sometimes find him . . . extremely useful."

Lucinda was not quite sure she found the man's smile reassuring. At that moment he looked very dangerous. "Oh." Her round blue eyes regarded him as solemnly as did the young gentleman's who pressed into his nursemaid's skirts.

Wynmalen smiled reassuringly. "Do you feel, perhaps, that it is time for me to call him off?"

Lucinda nodded. The Earl walked to the door, whistled shrilly, and put out a welcoming hand to ruffle the hair on the neck of the mastiff, who charged to his master's side.

With a whine of pleasure the huge dog flopped on the hearth rug. Then, with a satisfied sigh, he stretched out flat to rest from his labors.

Elizabeth realized that the situation in which they all found themselves was irregular in the extreme. Especially the comfortable way she herself had lounged in the scarred gentleman's arms. Obviously it was time she set all aright.

Sitting up very straight, and thus removing any notion that her person might again have need of the warm circle of his arm, she cleared her throat. Mentally she tried several ways of presenting an explanation, heaved a great sigh, and just plunged in.

"Permit me to introduce myself." She sounded

almost like the young gentleman she was pretending to be. She frowned.

"I am Elizabeth Chanders," she began again. "The Honorable Elizabeth Chanders, actually." She ignored the quirk of the man's mouth.

She was well aware that she must, in her present circumstances, look a figure of fun! Nevertheless, she firmly refused to be embarrassed by the necessity to which need had driven her.

She turned to include the others. "My sister, the Honorable Lucinda Chanders, and our half brother, Jonathan Mainwaring." She enlarged her gesture and said almost defiantly, "And our very staunch friend, Bess."

Bess gasped, then dropped a hasty curtsy, hiding her blushes in an upturned shoulder. Never before had she been introduced to Quality.

Wynmalen honored her with a sketchy smile. Tony's eyes remained on Lucinda throughout the whole introduction.

"I suppose I should explain my very unusual costume," Elizabeth offered.

There was that quirk at the corner of his mouth again.

"If you wish." Wynmalen bowed, the quirk back under control.

"Frankly, I think an explanation's a jolly good idea. Just what is a lady doing jaunting around the countryside in that getup?" Tony failed to keep the hint of disapproval out of his voice.

Elizabeth favored him with a scowl. "There is no male in our family to act as escort." She waited for him to understand.

Tony didn't. "There are Escorts of impeccable credentials for hire," he informed her stiffly. He sounded stuffy even to his own ears. Those flat-to-his-head appendages burned when he saw the pretty little blond Miss Chanders regarding him with tight-lipped disapproval.

"There was no time."

"We were running away from home!" Jonathan put in helpfully.

"Jonathan!" Lucinda scolded. "Do be still."

Wynmalen's eyebrow was rising.

"I can't be still. I'm hungry." Jonathan rubbed one eye with a grubby fist. "'Lizbeth, where is my dinner?" He yawned widely.

"Cover your mouth when you yawn, please, Jonathan," Lucinda instructed automatically. Then she blushed to hear herself, covering her own mouth momentarily with slender fingers in embarrassment.

"You don't have to show me how, Luce," Jonathan complained. "I already know how. I'm not a baby." He was the picture of offended four-year-old dignity.

Observing the scene from a comfortable distance, Wynmalen decided the muddle might be straightened out a little quicker if he took charge.

"It sounds to me as if dinner is in order. Allow me." Wynmalen moved toward the door.

"Oh, no. We couldn't inconvenience you. No more than we already have, that is." Elizabeth was flustered. She rose unsteadily.

Wynmalen, enjoying the blush that colored her cheeks, hesitated just long enough to say, "It's no inconvenience, I assure you. Though we have had our dinner, my brother and I shall be glad of your company." Then he gave orders for a meal to the maid their host had left waiting outside the door for just that purpose.

He turned back to the sisters with a smile. "Believe

me, Lord Stayne and I were beginning to wear each other a little thin."

He gestured toward his brother. "May I present Anthony, Lord Stayne."

Lucinda curtsied prettily. Elizabeth bowed her head graciously. She didn't think it would be quite the thing to bow from the waist, and she refused to even think of making a curtsy in her ridiculous disguise.

"And I am Wynmalen. Marcus Stayne, Ninth Earl of Wynmalen, to be precise."

Lucinda repeated her graceful acknowledgment of the introduction. Elizabeth, however, was frozen into immobility by his words.

Perhaps the blow to her head was making matters more difficult, but the usually articulate Honorable Elizabeth Chanders stood with her mouth half agape, struck dumb.

The Earl of Wynmalen, after duly noting what pretty, even teeth the Honorable Elizabeth Chanders possessed, cleared his throat and said, after a moment, "Well, ah, yes. Perhaps after you have had your dinner?"

This rather undistinguished sally was rewarded by a burst of musical laughter from the elder Miss Chanders.

Determinedly recovering her senses, aswim after such an overwhelming display of the Grace of God, Elizabeth told his slightly startled Lordship most enthusiastically that she would indeed be glad of a talk after dinner.

Having cleared up over dinner the mystery of Elizabeth's outburst of laughter, and extended his sincere condolences on the loss of her mother, the Earl settled down to ask why she had been on the way to his estate.

Preparing the way for just such an explanation, Elizabeth sent a mildly protesting Lucinda to put Jonathan to bed. She requested Bess to remain with her out of respect for the proprieties.

Obedient and obliging, Bess sat nodding in the shadows in the chimney corner. It had been a wearing day for them all.

Lord Stayne pleaded a previous engagement in order to give the strange young woman an opportunity to speak privately with his brother. Smiling his most devastating smile, he quit the parlor.

As the door closed behind the young lord, Elizabeth was given Wynmalen's full and courteous attention. She strove to marshal her arguments.

The decision to ask this rather austere man to take her and her two siblings into his home had been so easy to make when she had been standing, frightened of her drunken stepfather, in the dark hall at Chandering. Here in the candlelit inn parlor, however, she feared that she would be unable to make Wynmalen see the urgency of her request.

"Miss Chanders?" he prompted gently.

"Oh, dear. This was all so clear at home. And then in the rush to get away, I fear I have forgotten my carefully planned presentation of the problem."

He allowed himself the tiniest smile at her alliteration. "Take your time, by all means."

She regarded him a moment. "Do you enjoy an after-dinner cigar, Your Lordship?"

"I did, thank you, Miss Chanders."

Was that amusement in his voice? She sighed. "Of course you did. I remember the smell of cigar smoke when you gave me that brandy." She sighed again and looked at him earnestly. "It's just so hard to tell a stranger . . ."

"Your father trusted me." He paused, his blue eyes dark in the candlelight. "Can't you?"

"Oh, but that is just what I'm counting on. That I can trust you because you permitted my father to do so." She rose abruptly and took an agitated turn about the room.

His firm voice halted her pacing. "Sit, Miss Chanders. Then begin at the beginning." He rose and drew a chair out from the table for her. When she was seated, he took the place opposite her.

"Begin," he commanded.

Elizabeth took a deep breath and began.

CHAPTER
❋ NINE

Warm morning sunlight spilled through the diamond-paned windows into the inn's best private parlor. At the south end of the comfortable room, a casement stood ajar. Through it wafted the rich smell of the freshly tilled black fields across the road.

Raucous bird song pierced the morning for a moment, then was gone as the birds, lost in their ritual of spring, soared away, dipping and wheeling on the breeze.

Elizabeth, a young lady again in a becoming sea green gown that made her eyes luminous and brought out the red highlights in her chestnut hair, paced the private parlor restlessly.

She had not slept well, in spite of her assurance that Wynmalen would do what she had requested of him. She was apprehensive of his return from Chandering.

She supposed she'd settle down once the Earl came back from his self-imposed visit to Sir Charles. She was being sensible about the visit. There had been a split second during which she had felt resentment, as if he were checking on what she had told him, then another of unease, as if she might be mistaken . . . as if she doubted the evidence of her own eyes. Finally her common sense had come to her rescue.

She truly admired Lord Wynmalen for his fairness

in visiting Sir Charles. But, oh, *how* she wished he would hurry back!

The butler at Chandering was strangely reluctant to admit Wynmalen.

"I am sorry, sir, but the family is not at home."

"I am well aware that the young ladies of the house are not at home. I have just come from them."

The man's face changed subtly. Was that relief Wynmalen saw in his eyes? A very strange beginning to this very strange visit.

"I have come to speak with Sir Charles Mainwaring," he said with a firmness that brooked no denial.

The footman holding the doorknob shot an agitated glance at the butler. An imperceptible message was exchanged between the two, of that Wynmalen was certain.

He wondered just what was going on. "Well?" He let the man see his impatience.

The butler stepped aside, saying, "Henson!" The footman swung wide the door. "This way"—he glanced at the card Wynmalen had given him—"Your Lordship."

The startled glances he received from every servant they passed as he followed the man to his master continued to heighten his suspicion that something distinctly odd was taking place at Chandering!

Lucinda entered the parlor Wynmalen had engaged in a flurry of shawl and skirt and laughing little brother. Her face was flushed and her eyes bright from the brisk pace of the games she and Lord Stayne had been playing with Jonathan.

The child tugged her over to Elizabeth with enthusiasm. "'Lizbeth. Oh, 'Lizbeth, only look what Tony found for me!" He pulled at Lucinda's shawl, the corner of which was carefully gathered to hold some treasure that suspiciously resembled a rock.

Elizabeth gave him all her attention as soon as she had greeted Lord Stayne with a grateful smile.

"Show me, dearest. Is it a special rock?"

Lord Stayne's chuckle blended with Lucinda's merry peal of laughter, but Jonathan frowned them both to silence.

"No." He wrinkled his forehead in disapproval. "It's a turtle. It's just coming out of the mud to begin the spring, Tony says."

"Oh, my. Won't he dirty Luce's shawl?"

"Cos' not, silly. 'Cause we washed him in the brook."

"Ah, yes. I see." Elizabeth threw a smiling glance at the once gleaming top boots the young lord had sacrificed to a child's pleasure and liked him for it immensely.

"We must all catch flies for my turtle. Tony says he will be quite hungry after such a long nap. He slept all winter, you know."

"Did he really, darling?"

"Cos' he did. Tony says so."

Elizabeth lifted an eyebrow inquiringly not about the turtle, but about the use of Lord Stayne's given name.

With a smile that must be the delight of half the females in London, he reassured her. "I hope you don't mind. Titles can be a mouthful when you're young."

"Of course I can scarcely mind if you do not."

"Splendid." He turned to the child. "Jonathan, my lad. Do you suppose we men could postpone our fly

hunt until we have seen to a luncheon for the delight-
ful ladies of our acquaintance?"

Jonathan peered intently at his turtle. "I s'pose that
would be all right. He 'pears to've gone to take
another nap. He's closed his front door." He trailed
over to the window, staring intently at his turtle's
"front door."

Elizabeth turned to Lord Stayne. "Do you suppose
we should wait for your brother, milord?"

"Heavens, no. If he overdoes it, he'll have no
appetite and only grumble at us for waiting luncheon
for him. And if he rides sensibly, he'll come in
ravenous, so we'd do better to get our share while we
can, eh, Jonathan?" He swung the boy to his shoulder
and ducked with him to clear the door frame. "We're
off to demand some sustenance."

"What a likeable young man." Elizabeth beamed
her approval at his broad back.

"Yes, isn't he." Lucinda made it a disinterested
statement. She seemed less than taken with Lord
Stayne.

At her tone of voice Elizabeth paused, then asked
softly, "Lucinda. He hasn't done anything to offend
you, has he?" Elizabeth's voice was troubled.

"Oh, no, dear!" Lucinda was startled by the sugges-
tion. "I just got tired of all the village girls ogling him.
What a merry time the girl *he* settles on will have of it!
She'll need a very large stick to chase the other women
off!"

Chuckling, Elizabeth gave her an impulsive hug.
Both dissolved in laughter.

"And so, Marc? What did you discover at Chandering?"

"A disturbing situation, Tony." He drew off his

riding gloves and tossed them into his high crowned hat. This along with his riding whip he placed on a table.

Moving to a chair, he sat, his hand unconsciously pressed against his injured leg. Tony dragged a stool over, threw a cushion on it, and took a chair near his brother's.

"Join me?" He raised an eyebrow in invitation as he lifted his gleaming Hessians to rest lightly on the side of the stool nearest him.

With a sigh Wynmalen placed his left leg on the cushion and set to working the cramp out of his thigh. He grinned at his brother. "And to think I used to ride because it relaxed me."

"Brandy?" Tony suggested.

"Excellent idea."

Tony rose gracefully and moved to a table at the side of the room. A clink and a rattle, and he returned with two glasses half-filled with amber liquid.

They sat a moment, swirling the brandy, then each took an appreciative sip.

Wynmalen let his head fall back against the chair and sighed as the fiery liquid burned a trail from his throat to his stomach. Another two sips and the pain in his leg began to ease.

"Sometimes I can understand a man becoming a drunkard, Tony."

"My God, Marc. Is the pain that bad?" Tony's distress for him showed in harsh lines on his handsome face.

"What? No, best of brothers. Not me. Old soldiers learn to bear their wounds. I was thinking about Mainwaring."

"Why Sir Charles?"

"When I went to Chandering today, the servants didn't seem to want me to see him."

"Th' deuce you say. Why not?"

"The poor devil was drunk as a lord."

"And?"

"He . . . seemed totally unaware the children are gone. He seemed to be mourning the loss of his wife—but she died four years ago.

"He had no idea he was talking to a perfect stranger. It was as if he were deranged. A good bit of what he said didn't make sense. . . ." He frowned.

"Blasted uncomfortable for you."

"Yes. He told me he'd loved her since his youth, waited for her through her happy marriage to my Colonel, Viscount Chanders, then married her after she was widowed . . . only to lose her at the birth of their first child."

He shifted in his chair and half-drained his glass. "Damned uncomfortable, being allowed to see another man's agonies, Tony."

"Hmmmm." Tony crossed the room and brought back the brandy.

Marcus continued, musing like a man feeling his way through a maze of thoughts. "I sought to offer comfort by mentioning his fine son and was treated to an explosion of such hatred that I decided to keep our three houseguests simply on the strength of my desire to keep that child away from the man's malice. Believe me, I gained the utmost respect for Miss Chanders's good sense in bringing her family to me."

He struck the arm of his chair a mighty blow with his open hand, then lunged out of it and began to pace the room.

"My God, Tony. I could not credit my senses." He ran a distracted hand through his hair. "Mainwaring blames that fine young lad for the death of his mother. And if the things he mouthed at me today were true, he has spent much of the last year trying to cause the boy to regret the day he was born."

He regained his chair and sat forward in it, his elbows on his knees, to peer at his brother. "If I am to believe him, the two girls have been almost Machiavellian in their efforts to shield the boy from his viciousness."

"Good for them!"

"Yes!" He sat back in his chair. After a moment he asked, "Is Danvers still here?"

"Of course, you told him you had one more message to send to Castle Wynmalen."

"Well, I thank you doubly for sending for him. Not only did he serve to ease my mind by taking orders to the castle, but now he'll come in mighty handy in this situation."

"It's a good thing you had two footman with the luggages. You have so many irons in the fire, you need 'em for messengers."

"Yes—always seem to," Wynmalen answered.

"What do you plan, Marc?"

"I'll send Danvers to Triverton Park at first light tomorrow to invite our aunt to accept the chore of chaperoning two young beauties and a boy for the Season. I don't think Emily is the one to launch 'em."

"Emily!" Tony hooted. "Dear brother, you have a somewhat idealized image of your betrothed. I can form a perfect picture in my mind of her face at the moment of your suggesting such a thing to her." Tony threw back his head, and his full-bodied laughter rang through the room.

Wynmalen sat up rather stiffly. "I find your levity misplaced, Tony."

Tony looked at Wynmalen's Friday face, took another breath, and laughed all the harder.

Without another word, Marcus Stayne, Earl of Wynmalen, rose quietly to leave the room. Since Tony had decided to play the fool, he would spend the hour before dinner composing his letter to their aunt.

At the door, he turned to give his brother one last glare. Tony wiped the tears from his eyes, but, at Wynmalen's unspoken reprimand, chuckled and shook his head at him. No apology intended.

The door closed with unusual firmness.

CHAPTER
❊ TEN

"I have sent for my aunt to act as your chaperone. I feel it would be best if I did not divulge to her, nor to my brother, the full extent of your problem," Wynmalen began without preamble. His voice, even lowered as it was to guard the privacy of their conversation, conveyed his deep concern for her family and the problem she had brought to him.

Elizabeth looked up at him in the twilight, thinking again what a magnificent man he was. She walked on his right, and his unmarred profile was exceedingly handsome. Before his accident, or whatever had befallen him to scar his face, he would have been even more compelling than the young Adonis, Lord Anthony.

But it was his warm strength that made him so beautiful to her. Beautiful. What a strange word to use when thinking about a man.

She gave herself a good mental shake. Obviously she had been out of society too long and was therefore far too easily struck by a strange man's fine characteristics. Nevertheless, she knew she would choose Wynmalen to stand her friend over half a dozen truly beautiful Anthony Staynes.

She found herself wondering what had happened to Wynmalen, somehow knowing in her heart that his wound was war-related. It would be in the worst possible taste to inquire, but . . .

"I feel you have not shared with your sister the extent of your fears for her. Am I correct?"

She yanked her thoughts firmly back from wondering about the physical attributes of the man at her side and answered him gravely. "No, I have not. I feel that the situation is a very . . . unusual one, and I live in hopes that it will have changed before she ever encounters Sir Charles again."

His brow furrowed, and he turned his head to look at her. "Yes. One can hope. I think your course the wisest in any case. Your sister cannot help but go on better with an easy mind." He halted and clasped his hands behind his back.

Looking down into the lovely face turned so trustingly to his, he was having difficulty deciding just how much of his uneasiness about Sir Charles he wanted to share with her. Obviously, either the situation had deteriorated badly since Miss Chanders had left her home, or, he thought, assessing the purity behind those glowing gray eyes, her own innocence kept the full truth from her.

He found himself staring a little longer into those wondrous eyes than he had intended. Far longer . . .

From somewhere the enchanting song of a nightingale floated to them. With an effort he tore his gaze away and gently turned his companion back toward the now brightly lighted inn.

The maneuver put her on his left. On his scarred side. With a murmured apology he shifted his position to shield her from his disfigurement.

Elizabeth, still trying to catch her breath after the feelings she had experienced as the Earl looked so long into her eyes, didn't even notice. They continued on to the inn in companionable silence.

Upon reaching the welcoming doorway, Wynmalen bowed and gravely watched her as she ascended the stairs to her bedchamber.

His surveillance gave Elizabeth the distinct feeling that she was wrapped in his protection. That thought brought a little smile to her lips.

She was vaguely aware, too, that she'd had to make a small effort to separate herself from him at the door. Heavens! The man certainly had a most powerful personality!

Early the next morning the rattle of coaches and the clatter of the hooves of the horses being put to filled the inn yard. Elizabeth and her little family joined the Earl and his brother for a breakfast to be eaten to the accompaniment of soft neighs and jingling harnesses that could be heard even though the windows of the now familiar parlor were firmly closed against this bustle of preparation.

Jonathan was bursting with excitement, and Lucinda—having bombarded Elizabeth half the night with questions about their future—was all smiles. They were clearly excited at embarking on this new adventure that life was offering them.

Elizabeth was more solemn.

Wynmalen came to her side. "You're very quiet this morning, Miss Chanders."

Elizabeth didn't pretend not to understand his unspoken question. "I was praying that all will go smoothly." She met his eyes with her usual disconcerting frankness. "And that we will be allowed to live the next few weeks peacefully—without any unpleasantness from Sir Charles."

He admired her directness. "If I were a praying man, I would add my own to yours. Though I don't expect a problem, I must admit I judged your stepfather to be . . . unpredictable."

"I am painfully aware that Lucinda's and my own position can be somewhat justified. It is our having taken Jonathan from his father that may border on the actionable."

"And you fear that?"

She nodded.

Wynmalen had no answer that could put this fear to rest. There was a long pause before he said, "I can only assure you that I shall do my utmost to protect the boy in the event that Sir Charles should decide to recover him."

Elizabeth turned away so that he might not see the quick tears of gratitude that filled her eyes. "Thank you, Your Lordship," she managed in a tight little voice.

She prayed with all her heart that her stepfather's abhorrence of his son would cause Sir Charles to consider himself well rid of the boy. If he did not so decide, there would be nothing for it but to return to Chandering with the child, leaving her beloved sister safe with the Earl. But, oh, *how* she prayed that that would not be necessary!

After breakfast, as they waited on the broad porch of the inn for their traveling coach to be brought round, a curricle swept into the inn yard, occupied by two fashionably dressed bucks. The driver was skillful and drew up with a flourish.

Two ostlers sprang forward and held the horses while the men alighted. Both stared boldly at Lucinda, who blushed prettily and turned her back, ostensibly to talk to Jonathan and Bess.

"I say!" the driver cried. "If it isn't Wynmalen. And Stayne. Where have you chaps been keeping yourselves?" He rushed forward, his hand extended in hearty greeting. He shook Wynmalen's hand, carefully, with the air of one worshiping a hero, then fell with vigor on Stayne.

"Sanders! By all that's holy." Lord Stayne wrung his hand enthusiastically, "What brings a Bond Street lizard like yourself so far afield?"

"This new pair! Aren't they a splendid team? I talked Haversham into coming out for a long drive this morning to see if I was right to purchase them untried. Now the poor-spirited thing demands I feed him breakfast!"

The other gentleman patted his slight paunch and spoke: "Kennedy stuck his spoon in the wall, and nothing would do but that Sanders buy this pair from the heir. Body not even cold yet. Positively indecent."

Some of the light went out of Sanders's face. He looked uneasily in Wynmalen's direction. "Webster inherited you know," he told Tony quietly, his voice troubled.

Tony glanced at his friend's concerned face, and his mind leapt immediately to Lady Emily. Wasn't she once very fond of Webster? Before he could ask the question that formed in his mind, however, Haversham was speaking.

"What brings you to this out-of-the-way spot, Wynmalen? Thought you'd be at home getting ready to be leg-shackled."

Wynmalen smiled at his jovial friend. "The preparations are well in hand, I assure you. I have come here to meet my wards." He indicated the others.

Elizabeth was impressed for a moment by the way he handled their unusual situation, then realized that he had only spoken what was for him, now, the truth.

"Ah, coming to your wedding, are they? Good, good." The irrepressible Haversham bustled forward for an introduction.

Wynmalen smoothly performed the honors, and each sister had her hand kissed. Sanders approached and acknowledged them with a smile and a bow.

Elizabeth could not help but notice that his smile did not quite eclipse the troubled look in Sanders's eyes as he glanced surreptitiously at the Earl. She wondered at it with half a mind while she hoped with the other half that the distress she felt at the discussion of Wynmalen's imminent wedding did not show so plainly in her own eyes.

Surely the feelings she was experiencing came from her chagrin at foisting her troubles on the Earl at just the time in his life when he should be joyously free of all problems. Surely it was that and nothing more. . . .

When she returned her attention to the group, the two new arrivals were bowing themselves into the inn for their breakfast, and a coach was coming to the foot of the steps.

"'Lizbeth, this isn't our coach. That's not our coachman." Jonathan frowned at the splendid equipage for a moment, then was lost in the excitement of four perfectly matched grays, so white they looked like horses that had just stepped straight out of the pages of one of his favorite fairy tales.

"No, dearest, we had to send our coach back home." She stared momentarily at the arms emblazoned on the door of the vehicle. Somehow Wynmalen had gotten his own travel coach to come for them. Was there no end to his kindness?

"Are you gonna ride inside with us? Soc doesn't

have a saddle on. You're not gonna ride Soc without a saddle, are you, 'Lizbeth?" Jonathan looked at her with wide eyes.

Before she could reply, Lucinda hissed impatiently, "Shhh, silly. Of course she isn't! This isn't the meadow at home. And don't make everybody remember that Elizabeth rode here dressed as a man, for heaven's sake. Get in!" She gave him an impatient little push toward the iron steps of the coach.

"Don't shove. It's not p'lite." Jonathan scowled at her over his shoulder as he climbed in. "Come on, Luce. It's *loverly*!" His brief animosity was forgotten as he examined the shining silver appointments of the sumptuous interior. "Bess, can we sit with our backs to the horses? I want to watch where we've been."

"Yes, dearie." Bess bundled his few toys and favorite books into the vehicle. With a little difficulty she joined him.

Lucinda followed, sliding over the pale gray velvet seats to make room for her sister. With a last glance at the friendly old inn, and a last deep breath of the cool morning air, Elizabeth gracefully entered the coach.

The two men were to ride. It was a glorious day, and Elizabeth envied them. Having no sidesaddle, she was doomed to watch Socrates follow along after the coach, within her grasp, but quite, quite out of the question.

Wynmalen rode up to the window on a handsome bay stallion. "Are you comfortable?"

Elizabeth's sense of humor chased away the solemn thoughts that had held her quiet. Her gray eyes brimming with pleasure, she laughed. "How could anyone be anything but comfortable in such a magnificent coach? Thank you for your thoughtfulness."

He was caught for a moment in those extraordinary

eyes—so clear, so honest. He could read her very soul in them. He could drown there.

Under him Crytor sidled restlessly, trying to gain a position from which physically to express his displeasure at the presence of the strange liver chestnut gelding that was tethered to a ring high on the back of the coach.

The horse's movement brought Wynmalen back to himself.

Obviously the gray of his coach, the rich shadows of the velvet, the shine of the lacquered exterior merely enhanced the young lady's gray eyes.

Perhaps he would have a coach made and furbished with the blue of Lady Emily's eyes. He would consider it for one of his wedding gifts to her.

With this happy thought of his upcoming nuptials, Wynmalen raised his hand to signal the beginning of their journey to his home . . . and into the future.

CHAPTER
❋ ELEVEN

The drive leading to the magnificent sandstone pile that was Castle Wynmalen was almost four miles long. As the coach rolled closer to the castle, Elizabeth saw the banner that proclaimed the owner's presence blossom from one of the turrets.

Lucinda saw it, too. "Oh, look, Jonathan, there is the Earl's standard being unfurled." She pointed to where the scarlet and gold pennant snapped, brave against the bright blue sky, in the spring breeze.

Jonathan lunged to her lap and craned out the window to see. "Oh, how jolly! Now we have truly arrived, haven't we?"

"Yes, dearest."

All other comments were forgotten as they approached the foot of the steps to find a small army of servants awaiting them. Wynmalen and Stayne dismounted, and the Earl went to instruct his servants while his brother saw to the guests.

The men's horses were led away, as was a whickering Socrates, who dragged against his halter to look back at his mistress. Elizabeth gestured him away, and he settled down and docilely followed the two horses who belonged here.

She wished she had had the courage to go to him or at least to call encouragement to him, but she felt a trifle overwhelmed by the array of liveried servants scuttling around the coach, bearing their few things up to the massive open doors and into the castle. And she had thought Chandering was overstaffed!

She turned to reach for Jonathan's hand, and her eyes met Wynmalen's amused glance. Her ready smile lit her face.

Wynmalen moved to her side. "They are a little much, aren't they? My father has a very serious regard for his own importance. I've been unable to break them of the habit of puffing *my* consequence as a result. They'll calm down a bit once they become used to you."

He offered her his arm. Tucking her hand gratefully into his elbow, she chuckled. "I'm exceedingly glad to hear it."

They were laughing together as they entered the hall.

"Oh, my," Elizabeth exclaimed. The great hall soared up three stories, dwarfing them where they stood on its marble floor. Three of the walls were made of arches filled with windows in place of masonry. This made it seem as if the vaulted roof high above them floated, free, on pure light. "How very impressive."

"Hmmmm," he remarked noncommittally. "Castle Wynmalen is indeed nothing if not impressive. Come, there are parts of the castle that are almost like a home. If you keep to them until you are used to the rest, I assure you you'll be quite comfortable."

Lucinda, Jonathan, and Bess trailed after them, their footsteps echoing in the vast reaches of the great hall.

Jonathan, clinging tightly to Lucinda's hand, was absolutely silent as he eyed rank upon rank of suits of armor that stood at attention along the walls.

Lucinda felt as if she were making a mighty effort

not to gawk. Even having been raised in so notable a residence as Chandering had not made her proof against the almost oppressive magnificence of Castle Wynmalen.

Bess summed it up for all of them. "Gor, blimey," she breathed, bringing up the rear.

Arriving, after a considerable walk, at a lovely, sunny drawing room that overlooked what seemed to be miles of formal gardens leading down to a large lake, they were greeted by their hostess.

"Ah, there you are. Stone said you would be here in time for tea, and so you are." She advanced on them, a tall lady, full of smiles and streaming an inordinate number of ribbons from her lacy cap.

Before any of them had been more than introduced to the energetic Lady Esme Triverton, they found themselves seated with a cup of tea in one hand and a plate of dainties in the other.

Jonathan, for one, found this a most satisfactory state of affairs and wanted to know, "Are you *my* aunt, too? Wynmalen told me you was his aunt."

Lucinda said automatically, "Were his aunt."

Jonathan continued as if she hadn't spoken. "And he and Tony hab been nice to share things with me when I want 'em shared. Tony even gave me his turtle." He ignored the astonished look Lady Esme shot toward her younger nephew.

Suddenly his voice was breathless and shy, and he put down his plate to move closer to her.

The tall lady had to bend down to hear him say, "I can't help but think how nice it would be to have a loverly aunt who smells like verbena when she hugs you and has lots and lots of ribbons hanging from her cap."

She scooped him into her arms, hugging him close for a moment, then tilted her head and asked briskly, "Would you like me to be your aunt?"

Jonathan twisted his face up in the grimace that meant he was concentrating fiercely and was not to be disturbed until he had reached a decision.

Wynmalen watched, hiding his smile.

Elizabeth watched, too, and found, very much to her relief, that she liked yet another member of this extraordinary family with whom she had sought sanctuary for her own. Especially when Jonathan adopted her as his aunt.

"Do you like it?" Wynmalen sat his horse beside her, smiling.

"Very much. It's a beautiful view."

Her face didn't turn to him, and he was a little disappointed. He would have liked to see the enjoyment she professed shining there. In the week the Chanders had been at Castle Wynmalen, he had never failed to see just what Elizabeth was feeling in those clear gray eyes of hers.

"Oh, look." She gazed intently toward his home to where three tiny figures mounted on three tiny horses could be seen. "I do believe that's Lucinda and Tony taking Jonathan for a ride on your pony."

His rich laughter rang out. "I'm a little large for a pony, don't you think? Say rather, Jonathan's pony."

She blushed and turned her fine eyes to him. "You've been so kind. You mustn't feel you have to give Jonathan the pony. It is quite enough that he gets to ride it."

"Why do you object to my giving it to him, Elizabeth?"

Her eyes clouded a moment. "I don't want us to be a trouble to you."

"Is it that, or are you reluctant to feel in debt to me?"

"Oh, no. Never that. We are all three very much in your debt already, so that would be nonsense. I just don't want to—"

"Don't be afraid of being in my debt, Elizabeth. I should have to change a very great deal for it to cause you fear." He spun his stallion away from her. "Now come. If we ride hard, we can catch them at the south ride."

Elizabeth smiled and turned Socrates away from the bluff from which they'd been looking out toward the Castle. With a laugh she touched her spur gently to his girth, and they were off.

The servants had lit a small fire in the drawing room just to ensure against the evening bringing a chill to the tall, many-windowed room.

Tony, Lord Stayne, stood with his arm draped along the cool marble of the mantel, staring moodily into the flames. "This is Marc's last trip to London to finish the arrangements for his wedding. Then the happy event, then they'll spend a few weeks traveling." He scowled at the merry fire. "Then we will all be honored with the presence of the oh so charming Lady Emily."

"Tony, for shame! You sound as if you don't like her." Lucinda squinted at the embroidery in her lap, then held it at arm's length and looked at it again. "Do you think this looks all right, Tony?"

"No, it don't, Poppet. You always twist your threads." He went to Elizabeth where she sat in the warm sunlight flooding the window seat. "May I?" At her distracted nod, he took her work to show Lucinda.

"See. You have to keep the threads flat, or the whole work will lack the glossy quality that you do the job for."

"How do you know so much about embroidery, Tony?"

He grinned. "Don't ask, Luce. Don't ask."

"Oh, very well. I'd only hoped you would play the gentleman and give me a kind word."

"Too much to expect, my pet." He wiggled his eyebrows at her. "I am a man of action, not embroidery."

Elizabeth listened to their banter with half an ear, wondering why her spirits were so down these days. The Earl was kindness itself. His aunt was all they could wish. Everything about the Castle was perfect, including the servants. So why were her spirits so low? Surely she couldn't be missing Wynmalen to this extent.

Perhaps, like Tony, she was a person of action. Certainly the leisure she enjoyed here was a far cry from the active life she'd led at Chandering. "Do you suppose we have time for a ride before we have to change for dinner?" she ventured.

Tony was instantly enthused. "Capital. I'll race the two of you to see who can change and get to the stables first!" He was out of the room before his challenge faded, with two young ladies, so proper a moment ago, hot on his heels.

When the three of them hit the foot of the staircase at a run and shouting with laughter, Stone, and the two footmen he was instructing in the placement of a large potted shrub to one side of the massive front doors, stared in astonishment.

"Put dinner back an hour, Stone!" Lord Stayne ordered as he took the marble stairs three at a time.

"Yes, Your Lordship," Stone replied imperturbably, and glared at the younger of the footmen to close his gaping mouth.

Miles away in London, Wynmalen descended from his light traveling coach and eagerly ascended the steps of Simms House. The butler of his beloved's town house seemed surprised when he opened the door and found a smiling Wynmalen standing there, barely able to control his impatience.

"Good afternoon, Peterson. Kindly tell Lady Emily that I am here."

The butler hesitated, seemed about to speak, then turned to disappear down a narrow hall.

"Lady Emily will receive you in the green drawing room, milord," he said on his return.

He opened the door and announced Wynmalen, who had to remind himself not to brush the man aside in his haste to embrace his beloved.

As the door closed behind the servant, Wynmalen let his eyes devour his fiancée. She rose, placed her needlework on the table beside her chair, and extended a hand to him.

"Emily, it's been so long. How beautiful you are! Am I not the luckiest man in all England, my love?" He was beside her in three strides and had swept her into his arms before she had a chance to return his greeting.

"Ahh, Emily," he breathed between the kisses he pressed on her lips, "how lovely you are. How I have longed to see you . . . to hold you . . ." He brushed his lips across her eyes, then reclaimed her mouth in a masterly kiss, gathering her closer.

Emily stood in the circle of his arms and accepted his attentions until he released her lips and lowered his mouth to the base of her throat, reverently kissing the light pulse that fluttered there. Then she lifted her tiny hands and pushed lightly at his shoulders. "Wynmalen," she said gently.

He tightened his embrace and raised his head to kiss her forehead. Looking at her with passion-clouded eyes, he murmured, "My love?" and caressed her back with his strong hands.

She twisted in his arms and saw his eyes blaze with a fiery response. "Wynmalen!" she cried sharply as his parting lips sought her own. She shoved herself away from him and stood, one hand held up to forbid his advance, the other with its back against her mouth as if she would wipe away his kiss.

To see her thus was as if she had drenched him with cold water. Struggling to gain command of senses her rejection had sent reeling, Wynmalen could only stare at her.

Smoothing her blond curls back into their habitual perfect order, she turned reproachful blue eyes on him. "Really, Marcus. Did you have to behave like a savage? Please remember that this is, after all, an English drawing room."

Words of apology and reassurance rushed to Wynmalen's mind, but he refused to utter them. Somewhere in the depths of his being a warning flag was slowly unfurling.

His mind raced, seeking an explanation for the change in her. She had heretofore welcomed his embraces, sometimes with less than maidenly propriety. Could it be that Emily no longer shared his eagerness? Could the long separation of his war years have left her shy of him?

No, he had seen her several times right after his return from the Continent, and each time she had been receptive to his adulation . . . even encouraging it. He frowned in puzzlement.

"I am a solider, Emily." He spoke the words slowly, consideringly. "You must forgive my impetuosity." His eyes burned at her. "The last time we met, you led me to believe my embraces were . . . not repugnant to you."

"Much has changed since we last met, Marcus." Lady Emily's voice was cool. "Let's be seated that we may speak of it."

The smile that accompanied her invitation chilled him. He watched, narrow-eyed, as she chose two chairs facing each other across the cold hearth. He saw that she avoided the settee that had placed them in close proximity on his earlier visits.

Something . . . some deep, wary instinct for self-preservation . . . came alive in Wynmalen.

"Marcus, do you remember Roland Webster?"

"Of course." He kept his voice noncommittal, urbane. He remembered the man very well—a wastrel, a womanizer, and a coward.

Webster had used everyone of importance with whom his family could claim acquaintance to assure himself a position on the staff that was always farthest from the line of battle and had ended by selling his commission when that did not strike him as safe enough. What could that vermin have to do with his Emily?

"Well, Ronald has inherited his uncle's title and estates. He's a Baron now. And though his fortune is not as large as yours . . ."

Wynmalen lost the rest of her words in the roar of blood that filled his head. Numbly he watched her face. Saw the cunning expression in the blue eyes he had once thought guileless, eyes he would have eulogized if he'd but had the talent for rhyming.

He watched her dear mouth—the sweet, familiar curve of her lips that were now speaking words that delivered the death blow to all his hopes.

With a superhuman effort, he brought himself back to attention, only to hear her say, "And of course, Roland and I have loved each other from childhood. When my parents rejected his suit . . . he was penniless, you know . . . of course I accepted you. But now that he has inherited . . ." Her voice trailed off. "Surely you understand?"

She closed the distance between them and looked up at him meltingly. She smiled at him sweetly, appealingly, asking for his forbearance. "Surely you can understand, can you not, dear Marcus?" She placed a gentle, pleading hand on his sleeve.

The feeling that he had sustained a mortal wound and was only waiting to fall down dead left him. Suddenly he was infused with life brought to him by towering rage.

He glanced down at her hand and shook it off his arm as if it were a garden slug. Through the bile that rose in his throat, he managed to grind out, "Yes, I do understand, Emily."

He glared down at her for a long moment. Then, not trusting himself to speak further, he said roughly, "Goodbye."

He spun on his heel and made blindly for the door. His long strides carried him through it and to the front entrance. He refused to slow to hear her demands.

"Wait. We have to discuss a method by which to terminate our betrothal. Wait, Marcus."

But he had snatched his hat and gloves from the hall table and gone on.

Stung by his disregard of her pretty pleas, she lost her temper and taunted, "At least I don't have to steel myself to accept *his* embraces!" she shouted at him. "Roland is not disfigured and lame!" She screeched her fury at his retreating back.

The door vibrated in its frame from the force with which Wynmalen slammed it.

CHAPTER
❋ TWELVE

Marcus hurled himself up the steps and through the huge, heavily carved doors of Castle Wynmalen, leaving his distressed coachman to see to the blown horses who stood with drooping heads and lathered, heaving sides on the gravel drive.

All the long way from London, Marcus had alternated between a desire to weep and a rage to destroy. Now his fists clenched and unclenched only to clench again as he longed for physical release for the hurt and the blind fury that consumed him.

Stone, arriving in haste to attend him, was thrust roughly aside as Wynmalen stormed down the long hallway and into his study. There, he slammed the door with all his strength, glorying in the satisfying thunder, smiling grimly as the paintings rattled on the walls.

The key grated in the lock as he shut out the world, bending the sturdy brass with the force with which he turned it.

Pouring himself a goblet of wine and taking the bottle with him, he flung himself into the chair behind his leather-topped desk.

He propped his boots on the desk blotter, scattering the correspondence that he insisted his secretary always carefully place there.

"Here's to you, Wynmalen." He toasted the painting of himself in his regimentals. "You safe and *whole* painted bastard." He drained the goblet.

The wine bottle clinked sharply against the rim of the goblet, and a second measure followed the first, as he filled the study with his curses. When the bottle was almost empty, he hurled it at the painted man who stared arrogantly down at him.

The bottle burst, and the claret stained the man's white vest like a mortal wound, trickling down the portrait like life's blood.

With a snort of satisfaction, Wynmalen lunged from his chair and went to the mirror that hung over a long side table against the wall opposite the door.

In silence he stared at his face reflected there.

"You sorry bastard. You believed her when she said your scars were of no consequence to her." Turning his face so that his ravaged cheek was fully visible to him, he picked up a branch of candles to see more clearly the long white scar that ran down his face.

When he could bear no more, he put the candelabra down with great care and braced his hands on the table.

"You believed her," he whispered. "You believed you could be loved and lead a normal life. You believed it because she told you. And all the while she found you repulsive. *Repulsive!* You fool . . . Never again! *Never!*"

He hung his head, drawing deep, body-racking breaths, fearful that he might come unmanned and actually cry—fighting the overpowering urge . . .

He reared away from the mirror, caught up the heavy candelabra, and smashed it into the silvered glass.

From the other side of the door he heard an anguished cry. "Your Lordship! Milord! Be ye all right, sir?"

The concern in Stone's voice pushed him over some precipice. "Go away!" he shouted with all his might. "Go away, blast you!"

He seized the poker from its place on the hearth and fiercely began smashing everything he could smash with it. Over the tinkle of falling, broken glass, he heard Stone's footsteps running away from the study door.

Upstairs, Stone pounded on Elizabeth's door. "Miss Chanders, Miss Chanders, please, come quick!"

Elizabeth flew to the door, struggling into her wrapper. "What is it, Stone?" she asked, wide-eyed. "Is it Jonathan? Has something happened to Jonathan?"

"Ah, no, miss. The little lad's fine. It's the Earl, miss. He's come back from London a madman"—he spread his hands helplessly—"and I don't know what to do!" Suddenly Stone looked like an old, old man.

"Where is he, Stone? I'll come." She tied her sash as she spoke, closing her door softly behind her.

"God bless you, miss! Man and boy I ain't seen him like this, not ever. No matter how bad the pain was, no matter how hard it was for him to learn to stand on that leg. I been with him through it all, miss, and I ain't never seen him like this."

He led her to the study door, and when she turned startled eyes to him on hearing the clash and clamor in the room, she saw tears in his.

Turning back to the study door, she knocked sharply. The noise in the room ceased. She rapped at the panel again.

"I told you to go away!" His voice was so rough she hardly recognized it. "Go away!"

"Lord Wynmalen, it's Elizabeth Chanders. Please let me in."

Quiet hung in the air for a long minute, then, in a low voice that rumbled with menace, he made each word distinct and separate. "Leave me alone, Elizabeth Chanders. I've had all of your fair sex I intend to tolerate." His steely voice rose in strength as if he spoke while making a terrible effort, and an instant later there was a horrendous crash as something of great weight hit the floor.

Beside Elizabeth, Stone twitched and moaned.

In a flurry of silks and trailing ribbons, help arrived. "Just what is going on?" Lady Esme demanded, a small silver-mounted pistol in her hand, and her abigail just behind her, gripping a heavy candlestick as a weapon. "What on earth is happening?"

Elizabeth and Stone looked at her helplessly.

Lady Esme turned toward the door. "Is that you in there, Marcus?" Her only answer was the tinkling of glass.

"Well!" The word was a huff of indignation. "I insist that you behave yourself, Wynmalen. A fine way to behave." She drew herself up and in an even firmer tone delivered her awful pronouncement. "Wynmalen! *You are frightening the servants.*"

Instantly there was silence within the study. Then came the faint sound of Marcus's boots crushing broken glass into the carpet as he crossed to the door.

"You are right, of course, Aunt." Though the thick oak door remained adamantly closed, those outside it could hear that Wynmalen sounded a trifle breathless.

"No matter what, one mustn't frighten the servants. If you will kindly take Miss Chanders away with you and have Stone bring me another bottle of claret, I shall endeavor to behave as I ought."

Esme gave Elizabeth a quick sharp look. "He sounds sane, doesn't he?"

"Yes."

"Then let's do as he says." She turned to the butler. "Before you go for the claret, Stone, tell me where Lord Stayne may be found."

"He be in Lunnon at his club, milady." Stone was still so unnerved he forgot his usual precise English.

"Very well. I'll find a footman to go get a groom. You get the wine."

Stone started to hurry off.

"But Stone!" She called him back again. "Bring some chablis as well. Tell him he can drink his claret, but if he wants to throw wine around, he's to throw the chablis. Claret stains."

The two women paced the drawing room in turns. A footman had been dispatched to find a groom to send to London in search of Tony, and Elizabeth and Lady Esme could only wait.

"I think I shall go up and dress, Lady Esme. I'll be back in a moment."

She started toward the doorway, only to find it filled with the strong figure of Lord Stayne, still enveloped in his many-caped driving coat.

"Dear God!" Lady Esme cried. "However did you get here so quickly?"

"I came as soon as I heard the news at White's." His voice was bitter, his face full of anger and pain. "Alston came in and said he'd seen Marcus leave Emily's as if there were devils chasing him.

"Then a crony of Roland Webster's laughed and said she had probably told Marc she was going to marry Webster instead. I came immediately. Didn't even stop to challenge that bas—"

"Elizabeth isn't accustomed to the sort of language you would like to use, Tony," Lady Esme cut him off sharply.

"Yes, Aunt."

"An apology, if you please."

"I apologize, Elizabeth."

Elizabeth made a dismissive gesture with her hand. She would have been amused at another time to see the power the tall woman exercised over her two nephews, but tonight held no hint of amusement for her.

Tonight her very heart twisted in her breast to think what pain her dear friend Marcus must be experiencing.

She asked, "Did the groom reach you?"

"No, I met him a few miles down the road, and we came in together. He was in a bit of a state. Is Wynmalen badly off?"

"Well, what do you expect him to be?" Esme snapped. "You know how that faithless jade made up to him and led him along."

"He loves her, Aunt."

"Indeed he does not! I won't hear of it! He was infatuated with her because she was pretty and sought-after.

"A few endearing letters to keep him on the string after he'd become betrothed to her—naturally they'd mean a great deal to a man deep in the business of war. Then when he came home wounded and she managed not to shudder when she saw his face, her conquest was complete!"

Lady Esme huffed once, then set about to be fair. Reluctantly she admitted, "It *was* awful at first, when the scar was fresh and that whole side of his face an angry red and slightly swollen.

"And the other *ladies*," she hissed the word scathingly, "of the *ton* turned away when my nephew approached. Turned their backs, mind you!" She aimed this last remark at Elizabeth, as if explaining how Lady Emily could have managed to ingratiate herself with Wynmalen.

Tony shook his head. "That's as may be, Aunt Esme, but—"

"But me no *buts*, Tony. I won't listen to them!" Esme whirled and paced, then whirled back again and shook her finger under his nose. "Love is something you have for someone who has *character*.

"And that little bit of fluff never had an ounce. Wynmalen was her *target*, not her love.

"While he was away at war, that silly twit made a complete fool of herself over that nauseating Roland Webster. She *had* to keep our Wynmalen—after that nobody else would have her! Nobody with a big enough fortune and good enough title, certainly."

"He loves her, all the same." Tony's face showed his anguished concern for his brother, and Esme relented.

"Aye, of course he does, poor lamb. How is a soldier to know when a woman is true? Women so easily deceive, and you men are all fools."

It was an indication of the depths of Tony's worry over Marcus that he, who had made a career of proving the shoe was easily worn on the other foot, failed to take issue with her statement.

"So," Tony sighed, "what's to be done?"

Esme's shoulders slumped, and for the first time Elizabeth realized that she was an old woman. The realization brought tears to her eyes.

The tears weren't for Esme; she'd only been the

excuse they'd needed to betray Elizabeth. To make her admit that she cared more than she was quite ready to care about this family . . . and about Wynmalen in particular.

"Esme," Tony urged, "tell us what is to be done."

"There's nothing to be done at the moment but to let him drink himself senseless. And unless I'm very much mistaken, he's already doing that!

"As for the rest, I'll just have to think about it in the morning. Now let's go lie in our beds for what's left of the night. We'll need what rest we can get to face tomorrow." She turned resolutely away. "God knows there'll be no sleep," they heard her mutter as she left the room.

Blandings, forgetting, for once, to act the proper abigail, smiled wanly at Elizabeth and Tony and trailed after her mistress, the forgotten candlestick hanging from her hand.

Tony flung wide an arm, and Elizabeth walked out of the room and to the stairs tucked under it, her arm loosely around his waist. They were both so lost in concern for Wynmalen, that neither thought of the impropriety of it.

CHAPTER
❊ THIRTEEN

The morning light was as wan as Elizabeth felt. Gray clouds scudded low over the damp meadows and parkland outside the castle, and the overall feeling of the day fitted exactly Elizabeth's own mood.

Sleep last night had been out of the question, just as Lady Esme had prophesied, so she had been painfully aware of the effort necessary to put the drunken Earl to bed.

It had taken several footmen to aid Stone in dragging Wynmalen, alternatively vociferously angry and sullenly silent, up the grand stairway and down the hall to his bedchamber.

She had stood with her forehead pressed against a cool panel of her door, listening to his progress, aching to be of some help, powerless to go to him.

Then she'd done the only thing she could do. Whispering into her clasped hands, she finished a brief prayer and pressed her hand against the door as if to speed it on its way. Then she'd gone back to her bed, there to toss and turn until morning light.

Now, searching her mind to find a way to be of some help in this terrible time, she walked softly down the stairs. The first things to strike her eye were the decorations of plants and flowers, in various stages of completion, that Wynmalen had ordered placed throughout the castle to greet his bride. While none of the huge bouquets he had planned were in place, the shrubs and flowering plants that were to augment them were already in evidence.

Here was something she could do. She found a footman. "Please ask Lord Stayne to attend me when he awakes."

"Yes, miss."

She found the house disquieting with everyone still abed. In a strange way the atmosphere resembled that of Chandering, and she found herself wondering if another storm were about to break within *these* walls. Then she shook herself mentally and forced her thoughts to a less fanciful path.

Seemingly without volition she arrived at the door of Wynmalen's study. Hesitantly, she reached out and turned the door handle.

Inside, Stone jumped to see her enter. "Excuse me, miss. You gave me a bit of a start."

"I'm sorry." Then she saw the state of the room. "Oh, dear." She looked around her. "Heavens, Stone. Could one man do all this?"

"I'm afraid so, miss." The butler shook his head regretfully. "An extraordinary man in all things is our Earl. Never has done anything by halves not since he was a lad." He bent down to pick up half an expensive vase and sighed. "When he's himself again, he will regret losing this. It was his mother's favorite. Always picked the flowers for it herself, she did."

"Can't it be mended? Perhaps not made waterproof, but made whole to look at, at any rate?"

"There is a man in the village that does wonders with teacup handles. I suppose one might ask." Stone didn't sound too hopeful.

"Will you, please, Stone?"

"Of course, miss."

There were footsteps in the hall, and she and Stone exchanged glances like guilty conspirators. But it was only Lord Anthony.

"Great Scot! What a mess. Don't tell me you're trying to put things right, Elizabeth? Where are the maids, Stone?"

"I prefer to go through the wreckage myself, Your Lordship. Maids have a tendency to clean, not to . . . well . . . glean. I've hopes of recovering some of the room's treasures, sir."

"Good man. I wish you . . ." His gaze had been sweeping the room as he spoke. When he came to the portrait of his brother, he forgot what he was saying.

Elizabeth followed the direction of his gaze. The portrait was slashed across the lower half, where Wynmalen had stabbed it with the point of the poker, then ripped it with the hook.

"Tony."

"Yes, Elizabeth?" He tore his eyes away from the wine-stained canvas.

"I think the best thing to do would be to have the portrait removed and sent to London for repair immediately."

"Of course, I'll see to it." He started to leave the room.

"Tony!" She called to stop him. "It might be a good idea to have the decorations taken down as well, don't you think?"

"Best of girls. Indeed I shall." He paused. "Thank you, Elizabeth. We do need to do something besides mope while Marcus licks his wounds."

Elizabeth shook her head at Tony's choice of words and went back to her self-imposed task of helping Stone save the important mementos of the Earl's life.

Four footmen came with a ladder and went with the damaged portrait of their master, all with no words spoken. It was as if a funereal pall hung over all in the house.

Elizabeth was kneeling, searching carefully among the shards of the Chippendale mirror, looking for the last piece of a once lovely ceramic horse sculpture, when she felt an ominous presence in the room.

"Good morning, Elizabeth. Have you been reduced to the status of housemaid in my absence?"

She leapt to her feet, startled. Turning, she faced him, the pieces of the equestrian statue in her hands.

"N-No, I was just trying to save some of your things."

His eyes blazed at her, dark blue with chips of ice in them. The mouth she had thought so mobile and expressive was set in a hard line. From feeling foolish and startled, she went to feeling rather afraid. This haggard man was not her friend, Wynmalen.

"So you seek to save my things for me, do you? I am delighted to find you wish to be so obliging." He aimed his sarcastic words straight at her, as if he hoped to cut her cruelly with each one.

He stood looking coldly down at her, willing her to feel the weight of his displeasure.

Elizabeth felt like a rabbit—mesmerized. What had *she* done to deserve this treatment? Without taking her eyes from his face, she moved to the desk and put down the broken pieces of the horse.

Suddenly his fine nostrils flared with a sharp intake of breath, and his gaze became speculative. A decision was obviously made, and when finally he spoke, he said ominously, "If you are so determined to *save* things for me, I have a task for you that will save something infinitely more important to me than mere possessions."

He locked his hands at the small of his back and began to pace the room.

Elizabeth turned her back to the desk and leaned against it, clutching its carved edge with both hands. The solid bulk of the desk was somehow reassuring. And Elizabeth was in need of reassuring.

Suddenly she was afraid that having fled to Wynmalen had not been a very good idea. When he turned his cold smile on her, she was very sure it had not.

"Are you uncomfortable, Miss Chanders?"

She didn't answer. She knew that the question was more than a rhetorical one only in its tendency toward cruelty. She simply looked at him levelly and waited for him to speak.

"My brother is handsome and rich, Miss Chanders." He looked at her sardonically.

"Surely you don't expect me to take issue with that statement, my lord?"

"Indeed, how could you? However, for all that he is personable and amiable . . . You do find him amiable, do you not, Miss Chanders?"

"Of course," she said, a small puzzled frown gathering on her forehead. Whatever could he be getting at and why was he speaking to her as if he were a very poor actor in a second-rate play and she the audience?

"Personable and amiable. Yes." He took another quick turn about the room, his bootheels grinding glass. "However, my brother has an unfortunate propensity for creating near scandals. Anthony is a little unstable."

"He is young."

Ignoring her comment, with a brief scowl Wynmalen went on. "I made the comment to my brother not long ago that if I could find a sensible and steady girl to marry him to, I would do so."

Prickles of apprehension ran up Elizabeth's spine. She unclenched her hands from the edge of Wynmalen's desk and slowly rubbed her arms as if they were cold. Her eyes were wide with that same apprehension.

Wynmalen steeled himself against those eyes. Those eyes he'd once thought a man could drown in. How trite that phrase. It sickened him to realize he had ever allowed himself to think it.

"I have decided that you will make a most excellent wife for Anthony, Miss Chanders." He felt his teeth clench and heard himself add spitefully, "He is also whole and completely without blemish. I believe that counts very heavily with you *ladies*." He made his last word deliberately offensive.

Elizabeth's eyes registered the shock of the insult. She gasped at the outrageousness of his behavior.

How dare a gentleman discuss with her the body of another! And then to call her *lady* as if it were a title to be despised! Surely *he* had just taken all luster from the word *gentleman*!

His vile words had implied that she had, by deed, word, or even in her thoughts, indicated that physical perfection was necessary in order for her to form an attachment. How dreadfully unfair that was in the light of the feelings she had for him.

No more! She refused to allow this line of thought. It was a full minute before she came to grips with his words and formed an answer.

Hastily he said, "I am sure you are quite willing to oblige me in this."

He had not spoken quickly enough. Before his

sentence was finished, Elizabeth had cried, "You can't be serious!"

Her choice of words was unfortunate. Wynmalen stifled the shame that rose in him at his boorish behavior. Resolutely crushing the slight sympathy he might have felt for her plight, he said icily, "I am *quite* serious, I assure you."

He closed the space between them in a single limping stride and seized her arm in a bruising grip. "And if you expect me to keep offering my protection to your sister and half brother, I advise you to become quite serious as well."

His eyes blazed sapphire flames down at her. His voice grated as he told her, "Believe me, Elizabeth, you *will* marry Anthony. You have no choice."

CHAPTER
✳ FOURTEEN

"Oh, Elizabeth, dearest, whatever is the matter?"
Lucinda threw herself to her knees on the smooth,
newly green grass beside her sobbing sister.

"Oh, my!" Elizabeth sat up like a shot. "Lucinda.
Oh, dear, where ever did you come from?" Hastily she
wiped the tears from her eyes with her fingers and
sniffed once, fumbling for her handkerchief. Distract-
edly she ran a hand over her forehead to push her
disheveled curls back into place.

"From the house, of course, when I couldn't find
you anywhere." She took her sister's hand tenderly.
"What is it, dear? Why are you out here crying under
a willow tree?"

Elizabeth smiled a watery smile. "It seemed a very
good place to have a cry. Who would look for me in
this lovely green cave?"

Lucinda glanced around at the graceful branches
that trailed in supple arcs from the tree to the ground.
"Indeed, it is rather like a cave. It's also a *weeping*
willow, as you will no doubt point out next. But you
haven't told me why you are crying, and that's more
to the point than Wynmalen's landscaping, don't you
think?"

"I'm just tired, I suppose." She had no intention of
telling Lucinda of the terrible scene in the study. Of

Wynmalen demanding her pledge to marry Tony as
the price of his further protection of her family.

"Surely there is more to it than that, Elizabeth,"
Lucinda said sternly.

More? Heaven knew there was more. Wynmalen
had turned into an ogre. An uncaring, cold beast of a
man, and most of her tears had been tears of mourning. Mourning for the magnificent, kind, and understanding man she'd known him to be before his
fiancée had jilted him.

"No," she lied, her nails biting into the palm of her
free hand, "I think I'm just having some sort of
delayed reaction to leaving home so suddenly."

A tiny furrow appeared between Lucinda's eyes.
Clearly she didn't believe Elizabeth. But Elizabeth was
not going to ruin her sister's chances of a happy life
here at Castle Wynmalen by telling her what a beast
Wynmalen had been—saying that she would no doubt
be glad to accept his brother, as his brother was whole
and handsome. As if she had ever minded the fact that
Marcus was not. As if she had even considered for a
moment that he was not!

To her Marcus Stayne was all that a man should be.
Or, she amended, he had been.

She didn't even know this cold, angry stranger her
friend had become—this ogre who demanded her
presence in his study tomorrow morning so that he
could put the coup de grace to forcing her to marry his
brother. Hence her tears.

Elizabeth looked solemnly at her sister and knew
that what she felt about Marcus Stayne must never be
shared with her. She knew that, whatever it cost
her, she would have to convince her dear Lucinda of a
lie. She must lead her sister to believe that she *wanted*

to be Tony Stayne's betrothed. She must. Otherwise, how could Lucinda accept her sister's sacrifice?

These thoughts, and the knowledge that she could never share them, were the cause of her despair. This would be the first time she had ever attempted to deceive a loved one, and it was unbelievably hard to bear.

She could feel the hot tears welling up again. She jumped to her feet and extended her other hand to Lucinda, pulling her up to walk beside her.

"Come, I'm quite over my silly fit of the blue devils. Let's go see if Jonathan would like to go down to the lake and feed the swans, shall we?"

Lucinda watched her sister smile with false brightness and wondered how she could learn what the matter truly was, and how she could help her. Whatever the case, she vowed she would not rest until she had discovered the real cause of Elizabeth's tears.

"You're joking!"

"I have never been more serious in my life."

Tony looked at his brother, hating the ravages that the last few days had made on his face and general well-being.

"I want you to offer for Elizabeth Chanders." Wynmalen's face was implacable.

"For God's sake, Marc! She'll laugh me out of the house."

"I think not."

"Well think again. She regards me as . . . a . . . friend. A brother even. But not, most certainly not, as a prospective bridegroom!"

"She is an exceeding sensible girl."

"Oh, indeed! Dresses like a young buck in clothes a decade out of date. Gallops about the countryside

with her sister, a four-year-old, and one aging maid—
and that one a nursemaid—for protection, so she can
find, and cry 'sanctuary' to, a perfect stranger. *And* she
then picks a fight with a bully three times her size on
the way!"

"She didn't precisely pick that fight. . . . Tony! I
wish you to wed. You have caused me no end of
concern lately. . . ."

"Oh, for God's sake, Marc. I haven't done anything
you wouldn't have done if you had been here instead
of off at war." Tony watched his brother warily. He
really seemed serious.

"Nevertheless, Tony, I told you that I'd know no
peace until I saw you comfortably married to someone
of virtue and good sense." He began to pace, and his
voice grew bitter. "While I have recently discovered
that there is no such thing as virtue in a woman, at
least Miss Chanders has shown that she has family
feelings and good sense for the most part."

Tony opened his mouth to speak, hot words rushing
to his tongue. Then his brother turned to him, and he
saw the pain and sternness in his haggard face.

His intended heated defense of Elizabeth's character
and his own freedom died in that instant. Wynmalen
had suffered endless physical pain in the last year, and
now his hopes for a bright future with the woman he
loved had been dashed.

Why should he, Tony, deny his brother this single
request? Hadn't he found one woman to be very like
another on close acquaintance? "What the hell, Marc.
If it gives you any peace . . ."

Marcus looked up in relief. Glad to have the decision made. Now Tony would be safe from the pre-
datory parents of young hopefuls and married to . . .
to what? Had he really been about to sing the

praises of one of the cursed sex? He must be over-wrought.

"Yes, it will settle matters in my mind for the two of you at least." He turned away, but not before Tony had seen his bitter longing.

His back to his brother, staring at the vacant space above the mantel where his portrait had hung, Wynmalen clenched his fists and added, turning, "This marriage will make our position stronger in the courts if it should come to a fight to keep the boy away from his father, as well."

Tony was glad, at least, of that. He, and indeed, all at Castle Wynmalen, had become fond of Jonathan. If by the sacrifice of his personal freedom he might make future life secure for the tyke, then he would willingly surrender it. So be it.

"All right, Marc. How much time do I have to secure Elizabeth's consent?"

"I feel certain that if you ask her tomorrow evening, she will do you the honor of consenting to be your bride." He couldn't keep the acid from his voice, though his face was bland.

Tony sighed, receiving devastating insight into the feelings of the proverbial condemned man.

"I hope you know what you're doing, Marcus. I truly hope you know what you are doing."

Wynmalen merely clasped his hands harder behind his back and looked at him with bleak and bitter eyes.

Tony had been increasingly feeling the need for fresh air, so he turned neatly on his heel and left the study. With fervor he silently cursed Lady Emily Simms with every step that carried him away from the afflicted shell of a man that had once been his brother.

Elizabeth noticed the absence of footmen as she walked down the long hall to Wynmalen's study, feeling for all the world like a soldier reporting to the firing squad. At the wrong end of the gun.

She heard the tall clock chiming ten as she reached the door. Straightening her shoulders, she raised her chin resolutely and lifted her hand to knock.

Before she had rapped a second time, Wynmalen himself opened the door. Unsmilingly, he invited her into the room with the slightest of bows.

"Good. You're prompt." His voice was rougher than she had ever heard it.

He gestured her to a chair that had been carefully placed in front of his desk, and moved around the broad, leather-topped expanse to his own. She saw that his limp was worse than usual and knew he had done himself further injury in the destruction of his once beautiful study.

Sorry for the pain she knew he suffered, Elizabeth answered him gently. "Some of us have virtues. Promptness is one of mine."

He looked directly at her for the first time then. His cold eyes raked her face. "I suppose you mean to inject a note of levity into this matter. I can assure you, it is not the place for it."

Elizabeth's eyes glinted, but she kept her voice calm. "Believe me, I find it no pleasantry to be coerced into marriage, my lord."

"Young ladies are coerced, as you put it, into advantageous marriages the world over, Miss Chanders."

Elizabeth regarded him levelly. "I had never thought to be one of them, milord."

His nostrils flared, and his brows drew together. He felt like a lion cheated of its prey. Why the devil did she have to look at him with those seemingly honest wide gray eyes? Strive as he would to find it, he could see no guile there. Only a quiet, deep reproach.

Blast her. He'd been tricked once by a woman's eyes, blue eyes . . . and in a more beautiful face than Elizabeth Chanders's, and he'd no intention of letting it happen again. He had no trouble hardening his heart against her.

"The matter is settled, then. When my brother proposes tonight, you will accept him."

Elizabeth watched him, looking for some sign of the dear man she had counted her friend, but she found not one.

She took a deep breath. In the silence of the room it sounded almost like a sigh.

Wynmalen felt his jaw lock at the sound. Before he could wonder why, he was surprised by her next words.

Very quietly she said, "There are two conditions."

His eyes narrowed. "What? Do you not think my agreeing to house, feed, and clothe your sister, your half brother, and," he added with acid sarcasm, "one overplump, aging nursemaid for the rest of their lives, if necessary, sufficient?"

Elizabeth smiled a crooked little smile. "That is one of the debts I owe you, isn't it? The debts you assured me I had no cause to fear. Do you remember? Do you remember that conversation, Lord Wynmalen? We were on the bluff overlooking the castle, and you said you would have to change a great deal for me to be afraid of being in debt to you. Well, you are greatly changed. . . ."

He did remember that day on the bluff. The day he had been sure a man could drown in those luminous gray eyes. The day she had raced him, fearless and joyful, to the south ride to catch his brother and her family.

He remembered, and he hated her for making him remember. Then he, too, had been full of joy. And now . . . he longed to crush her spirit. To force her to share some of the pain he himself had to bear.

"Then perhaps you had better begin to be afraid," he interrupted, his voice harsh even to his own ears.

". . . But I am not afraid," she continued, as if he had not spoken. "However, I wish to add my two conditions as a further price for my compliance."

He watched with hooded eyes, wondering impatiently what she'd dare.

Elizabeth went on. "I will marry Tony under two additional conditions beyond your continued guardianship of my family." She waited then, determined that he would take part in this conversation.

After a moment, goaded into speech by her silence, he said, "And they are?" Each word was a separate, hard-edged attack.

His eyes burned at her, warning her. She'd soon see he'd not agree to conditions proposed to better her position. She was gaining one of the most desirable *partis* in the whole of England as husband. What more did the greedy chit think she could demand?

"First, I must be assured that Tony does not find the idea of marrying me repugnant. Second, I ask that my sister have a Season and be allowed to marry a man of her own choosing."

Wynmalen rose from his chair, looming over her. He glared down at her, angered at the selflessness of her demands, but she held her ground. Still those clear gray eyes reproached him.

He turned away to pace the room. Finally he limped back to where she stood. His expression was unreadable as he said, "Why do you ask for a Season for Lucinda? Why do you ask for nothing for yourself, Elizabeth?"

She frowned at him for a moment. "I have asked for that which I want most. You have only to answer."

"What if I say you must wed my brother merely to keep our first agreement. What then?"

"Then I shall, of course, keep it."

"What? No tears, no agonized protests, no feminine pleas? I'm disappointed, Elizabeth." His voice cut as cruelly as a whip.

"I do not understand this unkind game you play, milord." She felt ill with dismay that someone she had so admired would deliberately attempt to hurt her. Every harsh inflection of his voice caused her pain, as did her certain knowledge that he would only be more angered if he knew that—knew that she cared for him, wished to be his friend, and felt his terrible pain as if it were her own. Carefully concealing her feelings, she said, "I ask for your answer."

Her dainty chin rose even higher, and Wynmalen had the feeling she was looking down her nose at him. In some deep recess of his mind, he felt he deserved it.

"Very well," he snapped. "Have your own way in this." He turned his back to his paper-strewn desk. "Now I must ask you to excuse me. I have much work to do." Picking up a letter at random, he stared unseeingly at it.

Elizabeth, weary of his attitude and stung by this rudeness, said bitingly, "*With pleasure*, Your Lordship." Rising, she spun away from him and was gone in a rustle of skirts.

Wynmalen kept his eyes glued to the letter from his bailiff at Wyndhaven until he heard the door close very firmly behind her. She was overset. "Good!" he snarled aloud. Served her right, trying to add . . . dammit, *adding* . . . conditions to their agreement.

The fact that both conditions were for the happiness of others only provoked him more. Something fine from his old self tried to reassert its influence over his behavior. He put it down ruthlessly.

With a mighty oath, he snatched up the ornate bronze inkstand that stood on his desk and made as if to hurl it at the door so lately closed behind the girl with the gray eyes.

Instantly good sense reasserted itself. He placed it back on the desk and took a snowy linen square from his pocket to mop off the ink he had slopped over his hand.

He sternly admonished himself to ignore the fact that his hands were shaking. Shaking with some emotion he just as firmly refused to examine.

Instead, he told himself calmly that the inkstand had once graced the desk of a de Medici of Florence, and that he had, after all, done enough throwing of things to last one so-called gentleman a lifetime.

Besides, it would hardly do to further upset the servants.

CHAPTER
✳ FIFTEEN

London! Elizabeth peered out of the coach window at the huge, sprawling city. The noise and bustle swirled around them, and Lucinda almost hung out the window on her side in her efforts to miss none of its magic.

"Elizabeth, just see. Through there. Isn't that the dome of Saint Paul's?"

"Yes, dear. I believe it is."

Elizabeth smiled at her sister's enthusiasm. She could easily see that things would be better here in London. She wouldn't have to work so hard to dissemble, as there would be so many distractions.

In the country, with so little in the way of entertainment, each member of a household seemed especially aware of the moods of every other member. Keeping Jonathan and Lucinda in the dark about the true state of her mind would have been doubly difficult at Castle Wynmalen.

But here Lucinda was lost to the spell of the great city. By the time she was immersed in all the plans that Wynmalen had made, it would take little to avoid her questions, for, indeed, she would quite forget to have any.

Shopping, and soirees, balls and routs, even a promise of fireworks at Vauxhall Gardens—since he'd agreed to Lucinda's Season, Wynmalen was over-whelming them with plans for London entertainments.

He was adamant, however, that Jonathan spend most of his time at Castle Wynmalen. He declared that the air in London, loaded with coal smoke from thousands of chimneys, and the disease that existed in the crowds of its inhabitants were risks to which Jonathan would be exposed to only on special occasions.

When Jonathan showed his acute disappointment at this pronouncement, Wynmalen took him aside. "You must be a man about this, Jonathan," he'd said firmly. "Surely you know I've planned visits for you.

"The time will only seem long if you fail to keep busy. With Valiant to train and your pony to ride, it will pass quickly."

Peering out at the teeming streets, and the pale, ragged children that played in them, Elizabeth was sure Wynmalen had been right. She could see that Jonathan would, indeed, be safer at Castle Wynmalen.

As the coachman maneuvered his team carefully through the crowds, she came to another conclusion. Even ignoring Wynmalen's very real concerns, Jonathan also ran the risk of being overwhelmed by so much clamor and activity.

Thinking of Wynmalen and her brother, Elizabeth was hard put to understand how Jonathan continued to get along so well with the man who had become a person the rest of the household avoided. Somehow, they remained the best of friends, and Wynmalen's very rare smiles were all aimed at Jonathan.

"Oh, look, Elizabeth!"

"Lucinda!" Esme saved Elizabeth's answering her sister's cry. "It isn't at all the thing for you to go craning out of the carriage in such an unseemly fashion! Pray sit firmly on your seat and remember that you are a lady, not a milkmaid fresh come from the country!"

Lucinda, cheeks flaming, shot back against the squabs. Eyes round with contrition, she whispered, "Yes, Lady Esme. I'm sorry. It's jut that I spent all of my first visit to town at the *modiste*'s."

"Silly girl!" Lady Esme chuckled indulgently. "Don't look as if you will never enjoy another glimpse of London. We will be here for the next eight weeks at least."

Lucinda's smile broke out. "Yes. Isn't it wonderful?"

"Hmmph. I suppose that all depends on your point of view. From mine, it looks as if I'll be losing a lot of sleep."

She flicked a hand toward the window, where a pair of young gentlemen in a high-perch phaeton had removed their hats and were most earnestly staring in Lucinda's direction. The third, handling the mettlesome bays that drew the dangerously tall vehicle, could only hang on to the driving reins and color in frustration as his cronies described, sotto voce, the delights he was missing.

Elizabeth smiled, taking care she didn't smile in their direction, and patted her sister's hand. "Already you take London by storm, dearest. What a Season you shall have."

"What a Season indeed," Lady Esme huffed. "Looks as if the wolves are already gathering. And we aren't even unpacked yet."

But neither sister believed in the disapproval she pretended. Elizabeth smiled at her sister's pretty confusion and returned to her own thoughts.

Just now Lucinda was so thrilled with the fact that she would have a London Season that she habitually walked a foot above the ground. Her sister's assurance that she was happy to be marrying Lord Stayne was all that it took to liberate her from her grave misgivings about Elizabeth and Tony's betrothal. She was free to fly about making plans for the wardrobe Wynmalen had told her she must start amassing. That particular enthusiasm would keep Lucinda so occupied that Elizabeth would be safe from her questioning.

Elizabeth hated to admit it, but she was truly grateful to Wynmalen for distracting Lucinda. Lying to her would always be difficult. The very thought of attempting to do so caused Elizabeth pain.

The streets were wider now, the drays and wagons with their heavy loads and plodding horses that had impeded their progress gave way to more fashionable curricles and phaetons with their beautiful, high-strung teams.

The latter impeded their progress no less, but they added the thrill of imminent collision, as ham-handed young dandies were as much in evidence as were Corinthian bucks who drove with dash and precision.

"There is Devonshire House," Lady Esme announced. Both girls were careful not to crane out the window to look.

Tall, elegant houses lined these streets, and they began to pass small private parks, their wrought-iron gates locked to preserve their use for those who lived in the beautifully kept row houses that fronted the square.

Finally the coach turned into another very wide street and came to a smooth halt in the half-moon drive in front of a palatial house that must have taken

up half a city block. Indeed, with formal gardens
flanking it in military precision on either side, it did
manage to occupy the whole city block.

The block to the right of the mansion held two
homes, as did the one opposite it. The one on the left
also held but a single building, but it had only two
stories. Twining House—a legacy from Wynmalen's
maternal grandmother, Esme had said—was a full
four stories tall, not counting the attics.

In the center of the square there was an even larger
park than she had hitherto seen. It was neatly enclosed
by a tall iron fence that was broken in the exact center
of each side by impressively locked wrought-iron
gates. Three children played there, under the watchful
eye of their nanny.

The doors to Twining House opened, and again
Wynmalen's army of servants appeared. Though a
different army, their livery, as well as their level of
efficiency, was the same. This time, however, there
was plenty for them to carry, and, finally used to their
companion army at Castle Wynmalen, the Chanderses
were comfortable with their number.

Wynmalen, with his brother, had arrived only moments earlier in his own vehicle, but Elizabeth saw
that Wynmalen was nowhere in evidence. Tony, however, had waited for them and stood, smiling a welcome, on the shallow marble steps.

"Was it a comfortable ride?" he asked.

"Indeed, yes, Tony." Lucinda dazzled him with her
own radiant smile, her pleasure in the city giving her
face a lovely glow. "Oh, why didn't you tell me it was
so . . . so . . ."

"Ah, Poppet, because *sometimes* words fail *me* as
well," he teased as he offered her his arm.

Lucinda slid her hand into the crook of his elbow,

and the two led the way into the house, their golden heads bent toward each other as they chattered about the delights of town.

Elizabeth and Lady Esme exchanged fond smiles and followed the eager couple into the house.

Wynmalen was like a thundercloud all through dinner, and when everyone met in the drawing room later, his disposition had not improved.

Elizabeth, not best pleased with him in any event, found herself growing quite weary of his behavior. She hoped she would be able to squeak through the evening resisting the tendency, growing in her by leaps and bounds, to set His Lordship straight in the matter of manners.

Lucinda, always aware of tension in her sister, whispered to Tony, "Oh, I do hope your brother does not continue to be so abrupt."

"Why, Poppet? He's unaware, I think, that he is not the best company. I'd wager his thoughts are all on Lady Emily still."

"Elizabeth will not see that as reason enough to make those around him uncomfortable, I'm afraid."

"And?" There was a chuckle in his voice.

"Huh," Lucinda grunted, no thought of charming the man at her side. "If you'd ever been the recipient of one of Elizabeth's scolds, you wouldn't be so smug, Tony Stayne. They're all the worse for being so infrequent."

"If you are going to be so formal, Miss Chanders, that's *Lord* Stayne. Much frostier."

"Don't be silly when I am being serious. Elizabeth is a bear for the manners one should exhibit toward one's family . . . and one's servants, too, for that matter."

She pointed delicately in her sister's direction with her dainty little chin.

Tony was fascinated. "How the devil do you do that without dislocating yourself?" He tried pointing toward the fireplace and clapped a hand to the back of his neck.

"Goose! You gentlemen do the same thing when your cravat is too snug. Only you do it to the front."

No one had ever called the beautiful Tony "goose" before, and his eyes widened in mock disbelief. "I beg your pardon, but *what* did you just call me?"

"Oh, *do* stop being silly, Tony. I am truly afraid that Elizabeth is positively going to attack Wynmalen if he doesn't stop being so very unpleasant."

Tony looked at her intently. "I believe you are really concerned."

His answer was a scowl.

"Very well, my pet." He took her hand and drew it through his arm. Smiling the devastating smile that had made him irresistible to the ladies of the *ton*, he suggested with the air of a conspirator, "Let us go and see if we can turn him up sweet and save Elizabeth the onerous chore of lecturing him."

CHAPTER
❖ SIXTEEN

"How can you go on like this, Lucinda? Surely you are tired. I was fatigued to death two hours ago."

Elizabeth declined to be further fitted and retreated to a comfortable, damask-covered chair.

"I have never known you to be so delicate." Lucinda could hardly contain her own excitement. "Just think, Elizabeth, Madame Bertin was dressmaker to the Queen of France! How fortunate we are that the Earl is of such consequence. Else how would such country mice come to the attention of Madame Rose Bertin?" Lucinda looked as if she were in the grips of a profound ecstasy.

Elizabeth smiled at her, understanding her excitement. "Yes, dearest, it is quite exciting to be gowned by so illustrious a personage." She forbore adding that she was far more impressed that the French *émigrée* had had the good fortune to escape her native land with her head.

After all, the Terror had taken the lives of many faithful ladies' maids; surely the woman responsible for enhancing the beauty of the ill-fated Queen of France could hardly have been expected to escape the attention of Madame Guillotine.

Elizabeth smiled to see her sister's eager participation in the matters of her wardrobe. It was apparent that Lucinda had entered into the life of a lady of the *ton* with great enthusiasm—certainly with greater enthusiasm than she herself had ever felt. "How lovely you look in that blue, dearest. Have you a special occasion in mind for it?"

"The Abernatheys' reception, I think. Though I may wear the rose silk one for that. Which would you say, Elizabeth?"

"I think there is little to choose between them, as they are both monstrously becoming."

"All the things Madame suggests are most becoming." She threw a sunny smile to the elegant Frenchwoman, desperately desiring to be seen in a favorable light.

"Madame is pleased zat you find eet so." The *modiste* accepted the compliment as no more than her due and signaled forward a girl who held four more lengths of exquisite materials draped across her forearms.

"Here are four afternoon dresses zat I envision being cut. . . ."

Elizabeth stopped listening to the unending talk of clothes and wondered what Wynmalen had planned for them in the next few weeks that he had ordered so many ball gowns, evening gowns, afternoon dresses, walking dresses—even six riding habits for each of them!

Obviously he meant them to make an impression on society. Possibly from the backs of horses if the twelve habits were any indication! A week ago she would have been sure of his intentions. A week ago she would have put his great expenditures for their clothing down to his kindness. And, of course, she would have been obliged to temper his largesse with her calm, solid good sense.

But the new Wynmalen wasn't acting out of kindness. He hadn't shown the least vestige of that characteristic since they had left Jonathan waving goodbye from the steps beside the drive at Castle Wynmalen. Even last evening when Lucinda and Tony had turned themselves inside out trying to cajole him into a better mood, he'd lacked the kindness to humor them.

No, it was more as if Wynmalen were a general supplying his troops copiously for an especially arduous campaign, and for the life of her, Elizabeth couldn't fathom it.

She sighed and shifted restlessly in her chair. How much longer was Lucinda going to be fitted?

As if in answer to her mental query, Madame spoke. "Mademoiselle Lucinda has been all zat I could wish. Would zat more ladies of ze *ton* were of her so cooperative nature. But now fatigue is present in ze shoulders. Eet is not possible to continue further at zees time."

Lucinda made a moue of disappointment, then laughed. "How good it is that I have you to watch over me and call a halt, Madame. Without you I would go on until I dropped. This is all so exciting to me that I promise you I wouldn't heed Elizabeth."

Madame smiled as she directed her seamstresses to take away the half-pinned gowns and armloads of trim that had held Lucinda in thrall for most of the morning. "Go now," she told the sisters imperiously, "take wiz you ze swatches of fabric I 'ave supplied you and find ze fans and slippers zat will complete zeese ensembles."

She made little shooing motions toward Lucinda, then walked away, her gaze pensive, already thinking about new designs to enhance the loveliness of these two very beautiful English misses.

Lucinda stared after her a moment, then turned to her sister, her eyes brim full of merriment. "I do believe we have been dismissed."

Elizabeth smiled broadly in response. "And about time, too. Come, let us dress." She rose and moved off, untying the belt of her silk wrapper. Lucinda jumped down from her dais and followed to where attendants waited to help them back into their walking dresses.

The mood that evening at the supper table was lighthearted. Wynmalen had escorted Lady Esme to a friend's dinner party, and the two girls were alone with Lord Stayne.

Toying with his wineglass, Tony commented, "How is it that Elizabeth looks so exhausted and you look as if you have rested all day, Poppet? Did Madame make poor Elizabeth stand up all day being pinched and turned and stuck with pins while you lolled at your ease?"

"Unjust! I was the one standing all morning. Elizabeth spent most of her time at the dressmaker's sitting quietly, sipping tea."

"Is that true, Elizabeth?"

"Quite true, Tony. I fear I lack the proper instinct for acquiring finery. Lucinda took all the prizes for patience as well as cooperation from Madame.

"She is to be the good example held up to the young ladies of the *ton* to encourage them to stand straight and still. No doubt the ladies will thank her for her good example." Elizabeth's eyes held some of their customary twinkle.

"Tear her to tatters, more like," Tony said soberly. "Can't say I've ever seen the woman who enjoyed having another held up for a pattern card."

Elizabeth laughed, but Lucinda looked daggers at

her future brother-in-law. "Surely you are joking, Tony. Madame will not hold me up as the guide for anyone else's behavior, surely."

"Wouldn't put it past her."

"Botheration!"

"Now, Luce. You mustn't snap Tony's head off. He's only making conversation, after all."

"Then why doesn't he converse about something pleasant, for heaven's sake." Lucinda glared at the young lord.

"My pet! You wound me with your displeasure. Surely you are aware I am considered quite ornamental by some of the ladies."

"Ha! I don't hold with men who are better looking than the girls they know. They usually get by on their looks and never develop virtues or character . . . or in some instances, brains." She looked at him pointedly.

"Truth be told, I really haven't spent a lot of time seeking to develop virtue." He ignored Lucinda's pointed sniff. "But I do believe you will have to grant that I have character, my pet."

Lucinda cocked her head to one side consideringly. "Tony, to tell you the truth, from all the tales I have heard of you lately, I fear that while you do indeed have character, it is all of it bad."

"What?" For the first time Elizabeth saw Tony shaken from his complacency. Lucinda, however, pretended not to notice.

"Oh, yes. Today at Hatchard's I chanced to fall into conversation with several young ladies. The general opinion is that Elizabeth's marrying you will prevent you becoming one of England's premier rakes."

"Why, you little tattlebox. What do you know of rakes?"

"Enough to be glad you're to be saved from such a fate."

Elizabeth saw the red in Tony's cheeks and decided it was high time to rescue him from her mettlesome sister's teasing. "Lucinda, do you think you will wear the blue or the rose gown to Lady Abernathey's?"

"The blue, I think. Though it's a difficult choice." She stood precipitously, pushing her chair back, taking her footman by surprise. He moved immediately to grasp the back of the teetering chair, shooting a look toward Beamish, then quailing under the butler's steady glare.

"Come help me decide, Tony."

For a moment Lord Stayne sat speechless. Finally he found his tongue and managed, "Poppet! A gentleman does not trot off to a lady's bedchamber to help her select her gown."

"What a rapper! Lady Carlisle has a cicisbeo who even tells her how to have her dresser style her hair. Besides, I doubt *I* could harm *your* reputation."

"Lucinda!" Elizabeth found herself shocked. Where in the world had her baby sister learned such a thing? "Just who were these young ladies that you met at Hatchard's?"

She signaled the footman to reseat her sister. He did this by shoving the chair against the back of Lucinda's knees until she plopped onto the seat, then forced the chair back to the table.

Beamish, aware that the young footman was new and flustered by his lady's standing without his assistance, pretended to be looking in another direction.

Lucinda named the girls who had spoken to her in Hatchard's, and Tony slapped his forehead and groaned.

Elizabeth's gray eyes widened. If their identity could wrest a groan from the habitually unshockable Lord Stayne, she knew she had cause for alarm. "Who are they, Tony?"

"Only the four fastest girls in the *ton*—Old Haveren's get. If their father wasn't a Duke, they'd be welcome nowhere. As it is, the highest sticklers look right through 'em. All four of 'em."

Elizabeth turned to Lucinda before Tony could elaborate, as he was obviously about to do, on the antics of the Duke's four daughters. "Lucinda. Please tell me that you won't have anything further to do with these girls until I have more knowledge of them."

Lucinda looked mulish.

"Better not, *chère enfant terrible*," Tony cautioned. "You'll find yourself beyond the pale if you're not careful. And *your* father was only a Viscount, so that won't pull you out of the suds."

"How very silly! They are just perfectly harmless gossipy girls."

"Poppet, they ain't the thing, I tell you."

"Oh, very well, Tony." Lucinda gave a great sigh. "I suppose I shall have to listen to you until I learn how to go on."

Tony looked indignantly at Elizabeth, who tried to smooth his ruffled feelings. "It might be a good idea always to consider Tony's advice, dear. After all, no matter how well you learn to get along in society, the benefit of Tony's longer acquaintance with the *beau monde* will still be of great value to you."

Lucinda looked at Elizabeth scornfully. "Gammon," she said distinctly.

"I say. This is very much like the child who hopes to catch up in age to an older one, isn't it?" Tony drew down his brows at her.

"True, I shall never overtake you in years, Tony, but I should certainly hope I shall overtake you in good sense. *I* shall certainly not rush around trying to sully *my* reputation, as you seem to have done."

Tony's mouth fell agape.

"Lucinda!" Elizabeth was appalled at her sister's want of manners.

Lucinda turned a bland face to her. "Well, no one will ever accuse me of being a rake. You can count on it!" Her golden curls bounced with the vehemence of her confirming nod.

Tony got his mouth shut in spite of the odds against it. Two of the footmen found it necessary to put white-gloved hands up to twitching lips to hide their hard-fought smiles.

Finally Tony sputtered, "Too right they won't! Only *men* can be rakes, my young addlepate."

Lucinda brought him up all standing with a single word. "Why?"

Elizabeth choked and put her napkin up to her mouth. After a moment, eyes suspiciously bright, she lowered the napkin, cleared her throat, and said, "Dearest, Ladies, simply because they *are* Ladies, would never behave in a questionable manner. Also I believe that you will find that the term *rake*"—she threw her betrothed an apologetic glance—"is only applied to gentlemen."

"Hmmph. Can't see that they *are* gentlemen if their behavior is questionable." Her darkling regard rested oppressively on Tony.

Tony reddened and sought words frantically, his front teeth showing in something remarkably like a snarl.

Elizabeth looked from one to the other in utter amazement. The fashionable, Adonis-like Lord Stayne looked like a belligerent child, and her own dear sister rather like an angry kitten—all puffed up hissing and looking for an opportunity to claw.

Heavens! Elizabeth thought, and slipped gently into the breech. "There is a different standard for the conduct of gentlemen, dear."

Lucinda whipped her head around to stare at Elizabeth. "Why?"

Beamish succumbed to a fit of coughing. The footmen kept their eyes on the butler until it subsided, leaving only a hint of color in his cheeks.

Elizabeth was relieved to hear Lucinda plunge on without waiting to extract an answer to her query.

"Why should they be allowed license when *I* shall not be allowed the slightest misstep? Look at what is happening to me already. All I did was repeat what some perfectly nice girls had said to me, and both of you are ready to come down hard on me. But Tony can run about the countryside—"

"Lucinda!" Tony's roar shook the chandelier as he sprang to his feet to lean across the table in outrage. His footman righted his fallen chair, then riveted his gaze on the ceiling.

Tony shook the stiffened index finger of his right hand at Lucinda and raged, "You will always be in the soup, miss, for you've less an idea how to go on than a certified looby!"

"I am obviously not the only one in the soup."

"Eh?" Tony was bewildered by her look of calm superiority. Chit didn't even flinch.

"Your cuff, Lord Stayne," she said with frosty disdain. "Your left cuff is in your soup."

This last was simply too much for Elizabeth. "Pray excuse me," she gasped. Rising hastily, she fled the room, leaving the two youngsters to battle it out.

Merry peals of laughter floated back to the dining room from the hall.

Elizabeth's footman looked around the dining room in triumph. He alone had not been taken unawares. Only he had managed to pull his chair back before its occupant toppled it.

CHAPTER

❈ SEVENTEEN

Elizabeth wasn't feeling quite as merry the next evening. As a matter of fact, both she and Lucinda were feeling a little out of sorts.

The Earl came home just in time to join them at the table. He completely ignored the tantalizing aroma of the turtle soup Aunt Esme had ordered to make up for her absence, cast one disapproving glance over them, and seemed to be seized with apoplexy.

In a strangled voice he demanded, "Just what do you think you are doing in those gowns?"

One of his eyebrows seemed to be trying to merge with his hairline, and his eyes blazed at the girls as if they had dressed especially to annoy him—and from the dustbin at that.

Elizabeth struggled not to be offended by the harshness of his tone, and Lucinda simply sat, her blue eyes wide with astonishment.

"We are eating dinner, Your Lordship," Elizabeth chanced, stating the obvious. "Is there some other matter you wish us to turn our attention upon?"

"It's *Wednesday*!" He spoke with firmness and looked at her pointedly.

Elizabeth was at a loss as to what Wynmalen could be getting at. Regarding him in a puzzled fashion, she waited for him to enlighten them.

When he did not, she ventured, "Should we forgo the evening meal on a Wednesday, milord?"

"Dammit, Elizabeth, don't be obtuse!" He ripped the words out in a furious string. Obviously he thought her a lackwit.

Elizabeth, further angered by his use of profanity in Lucinda's presence, snapped, "If you would be so kind as to make your point, if indeed you have one, *you* might be spared the annoyance of *my* being obtuse, Wynmalen." Two bright spots of color flamed in her cheeks, and her eyes lit with the light of battle.

Lucinda rolled her eyes to the ceiling and wondered why Lady Esme had to take Tony and run off to dine with an old crony on this night of all nights.

Wynmalen glared at the two empty places at the table. "Where are they?"

He was demanding again, not inquiring, and Elizabeth had had quite enough of his unacceptable behavior. All sweetness she asked, "Where are whom, milord?"

"Tony and the Aunt, of course."

"I imagine they had a premonition of your mood and decided this would be an excellent time to absent themselves from your table."

Wynmalen's mouth dropped open. The chit was insulting him at his own table!

Elizabeth went bitingly on. "I only wish we shared their clairvoyance, for then *we* could have been gone as well." Her clear gray eyes met his unflinchingly.

Beamish, supervising the footmen from his place at the sideboard, choked slightly.

His Lordship's lips tightened as he absorbed her jibe. Then, with marked reluctance he said, "Perhaps I have been a bit sharp. Pray forgive me."

"Certainly, Your Lordship," Elizabeth answered,

being very sure her voice held exactly the same uncaring, perfunctory tone he had used. There, she thought. Let him wonder if he will *ever* be excused for behaving so shabbily. Heaven knows he doesn't deserve to be.

Marcus gave her a look as sour as her own thought, shook out his napkin, and, with majestic deliberation, turned his attention to his cooling soup.

After a moment Lucinda, who was dying of curiosity, could contain herself no longer. "Why is its being Wednesday so significant?"

"Almack's is Wednesday," Marcus told her as if instructing the village idiot, his blue eyes icy.

"Famous! *That's* why you asked about our gowns. We are to go to Almack's. One wears white to Almack's!" She turned her beaming face to her sister. "Isn't it splendid, Elizabeth? Almack's. I have longed to go there forever."

Elizabeth, still irked at Wynmalen's behavior, commented quietly, "I thought vouchers to Almack's were always difficult to procure, but especially so this late in the Season." She fixed him with her gaze.

"True. But Lady Jersey is an old friend of mine."

"Oh, how perfectly splendid." Lucinda was aglow with eagerness. "What shall we wear? When do we leave?"

"Lucinda, pray calm yourself. I'm sure His Lordship will give us that information in *plenty* of time." Acid dripped from her words.

Wynmalen had the grace to look disconcerted. He should not have neglected to give the Chanderses advance warning of the ball at Almack's. He regretted his next words as soon as they were out of his mouth. "But, blast it. Everybody knows that Almack's is on Wednesday."

"How very nice for everybody. But won't it be a dreadful squeeze?" Elizabeth inquired overbrightly.

"No more so than usual, I'd say." His voice was wary. There was no doubt in his mind that he was for it now. He'd seen the stubborn challenge in Elizabeth's eyes. Just what would the little minx come up with? "Why do you ask?"

"Well, what with *every*one knowing the ball is on Wednesday, and *every*one knowing they are invited—"

"Dash it, Elizabeth, I didn't say everyone was invited. Everyone most positively is not invited. That's the whole point of Almack's. As you know quite well, vouchers must be procured."

"Ah, but how else were we to know we were invited? You did expect *us* to know we were invited, did you not?" she asked with deceptive mildness.

The Earl's face flushed at the hit. "Touché," he bit out. "Very well," he went on manfully, determined not to behave badly at this, the second time he had been brought to book by Elizabeth in a single evening. "Please accept my apologies for assuming that you knew I'd procure vouchers to Almack's for you."

"Of course." Elizabeth inclined her head in graceful acceptance of his apology.

The Earl, strangely reluctant to quit while he was ahead, said, "I'd be willing to wager Tony knew it was Wednesday. That's why he shabbed off with Aunt Esme to her friend's. He has no more taste for stale cake and weak punch than I."

"Am I to take it that Tony will not put in an appearance this evening?" Elizabeth wondered in alarm if Wynmalen expected them to go unescorted to the ballroom.

"I think we can safely assume that Lord Stayne will

be distinguished by his absence this evening." He scowled at the plate Beamish placed in front of him, wondering why the smells emanating from the excellently prepared food no longer tempted his palate. Had not, truth to tell, for weeks.

Suddenly the reason for Elizabeth's question dawned on him. "I shall escort you tonight."

Lucinda wondered why it sounded like such an unpleasant chore. For her part, she was more than eager to see the famous rooms at Almack's and only a little apprehensive of meeting the Patronesses. Especially Lady Jersey, whom she knew wielded great power in the social world.

She looked from Elizabeth's carefully bland face to the slightly angry one of the Earl. Because she could not think of a word to contribute, the three of them finished the meal in unblemished silence.

Almack's was everything Lucinda had expected it to be. Elizabeth watched with a near-maternal pride as her sister filled her dance card almost immediately.

The young men quickly flocked to be presented to this newest diamond, come so late in the Season to brighten it for them.

Nor was Elizabeth's card empty, by any means. After their introduction to the Patronesses by Wynmalen, both girls were besieged by admirers.

Wynmalen had gracefully explained that his Aunt was sponsoring his wards in their come-out, but as she'd found she had a previous engagement, he was substituting for her this evening. If the Patronesses found it irregular, Elizabeth had not been able to discover it as she'd watched them in conversation with the sardonic Earl.

When he'd finished his leisurely chat with these

great ladies who had conceived the idea for the balls
and who ruled with tiny iron hands the proceedings at
Almack's, he'd led Lucinda and her a little distance
away. There he stood casually by them, looking more
than slightly bored.

The young bucks were undecided as to whether
they wanted to talk of their horses with the Earl or to
dance with his very pretty wards. For whichever
reason, they came over, and the threesome from
Twining House was soon surrounded by a small
crowd of gentlemen.

Elizabeth was amused to see that their dilemma was
instantly solved by one closer look at Lucinda. She had
to admit in all fairness, however, that their instant
success was, in a large measure, attributable to having
such a pink of the *ton* as their escort.

Elizabeth's pleasure in their acceptance was
dimmed because she'd noticed that Wynmalen's manner seemed decidedly more intimate when he talked
with Sally Jersey than when he spoke with the other
Patronesses. Elizabeth wondered at it, then let it pass.
After all, Wynmalen was really no concern of hers.
Not *this* Wynmalen, at any rate.

That caustic thought brought a picture of a laughing
face full of kindness. His face. His no more. Her heart
twisted with the strength of the longing she felt to see
that dear countenance again.

She fought a feeling of hostility for the man that had
removed him from her acquaintance. The fact that
they were one and the same only made her more
perplexed.

"Our dance, is it not?"

Elizabeth turned from her bitter musings to find a
tall youth with a plain but friendly face waiting
expectantly. Smiling, she gave him her hand and, in

concentrating to follow the dance, forgot her unhappiness.

The evening passed pleasantly for the Chanders sisters, though Elizabeth worried that Lucinda would dance through her silk slippers. Then, just before eleven, just before the doors to Almack's would be closed to all comers, a small party entered.

Elizabeth happened to be standing next to Wynmalen, having begged to be allowed to rest for just one set. Turning to ask him if he knew who the handsome couple in the lead were, she saw him suddenly stiffen.

In a flash of intuition, Elizabeth knew the exquisite creature hanging a bit too obviously on her escort's arm was none other than Wynmalen's Lady Emily Simms.

Clad in a dampened muslin gown that clung to and defined every line of her perfect figure, she was easily one of the most beautiful women present. No wonder losing her was such a blow to Wynmalen. And she was deliberately bringing her party their way!

Without thinking, Elizabeth moved to stand nearer Marcus. He made as if to turn away, but she slipped her arm through his and held him in his place. Through his sleeve she felt the iron-hard muscles in his arm, and as if they were of one mind, she felt the incredible hurt flooding him.

She saw the smug triumph on the face of the woman approaching and dug her fingers into Wynmalen's arm. Smiling brightly up into his face, she commanded fiercely, "Laugh with me, Marcus."

He looked at her, astonishment erasing the pain of the moment before. He looked at her as if she'd taken leave of her senses.

Under cover of her laughter she taunted, "Coward.

Faint Heart. Do you so easily concede victory to the enemy on a real battlefield?''

He rounded on her then and moved violently to shake her from his arm, but she used the movement to swing herself against him. "Marcus, I have not been given permission to waltz."

She laughed gaily, willing him to keep his gaze on her. He did. Incredulously. Clearly he thought she was run mad!

Rather than permit her to plaster herself against his shirtfront, he stopped trying to escape her. Understanding at last what she sought to accomplish, he smiled stiffly down at her. He would play her game with his lips, but his eyes burned resentfully.

"I'd forgotten, my dear. You waltzed so well last evening at home."

Lady Emily stopped and stared, her blue eyes wide with shock. Wynmalen, far from being shattered by her presence with her beloved Roland, was actually enjoying a mild flirtation with the chit who was his *own brother's betrothed*.

She was crestfallen, and if the other two couples had not pressed on, she would have turned away from her prey.

The next few moments were passed in a flurry of introductions. Marcus was stiff, but the auburn-haired beauty at his side charmed the newcomers, giving them no time to remark it.

"What a lovely gown, Miss Everett. You must give me the name of your *modiste*." And before the flattered Miss Everett could reply, "Your hair is beautifully arranged, Miss Smythe-Patterson! I don't suppose I could prevail upon you to tell me who styled it?"

Before the highly gratified Miss Smythe-Patterson could respond, Elizabeth gushed on. "No, of course you won't. It was bad of me, a perfect stranger, to ask you, when one can see you have not even disclosed his name to your friend."

She looked pointedly at Lady Emily's hair, seemed to realize she had put a foot wrong, and clapped a repentant hand over her mouth. Round-eyed, she begged forgiveness.

"Oh, I am *so* sorry. I didn't mean you are not lovely, Lady Emily. Why, anyone as beautiful as you can easily carry off an unattractive arrangement of the hair. I mean, just look how well you wear that awful gown. . . . Oh, dear"—Elizabeth fell to wringing her hands—"I am so *dreadfully* sorry. I seem to be saying all the wrong things.

"*Do*, I beg you, forgive me. I am quite nervous. It is my first time at Almack's in over four years, and I am further undone to have as my escort one of England's heroes."

"Elizabeth!" Wynmalen broke into her prattle. "I believe this is our dance." He swept Lady Emily's friends with a glance. "Pray excuse us," he murmured, and firmly took a still-apologizing Elizabeth onto the floor.

The smile she threw back to the group changed subtly as he distanced them from her victim. From bewildered apology it changed to self-satisfied triumph. "Harpy," she breathed with quiet condemnation.

Her smile became quite genuine as she saw the highly flustered Lady Emily and her friends bidding their hostesses farewell. Their hasty departure, led by an infuriated Lady Emily, caused her to laugh out loud.

All Wynmalen could find to say was "Good God!"

CHAPTER

❋ EIGHTEEN

Elizabeth saw the sweat beading Wynmalen's fore-head and heard him breathing heavily from the effort it cost him to dance even so briefly. The instant the door closed behind Lady Emily's party, she literally dragged him to a chair.

Gallantly she stood between him and the curious eyes of the dancers, braving even his hateful glare to protect him from their gaze. Her courage failed her, however, the moment he was recovered enough from the pain his leg was giving him to speak.

When he carefully replaced his handkerchief in his pocket, she made one quick appraisal of his handsome face to be sure he could do without her in her role as screen and, as his glinting blue eyes caught hers, took to her heels.

Other than the music and the gay chatter of the dancers, the rest of the evening passed quietly for Elizabeth. *Very* quietly for Elizabeth where Wynmalen was concerned. For he watched her—his face coldly set—the remainder of the time they were at Almack's and never said one word.

When at last the ball was over, and they waited for their carriage at the crowded entrance, reminders of future engagements were made, and fresh invitations proffered. Then, finally, everyone departed for home.

By the time Wynmalen had settled the girls in his light town coach, he had found his voice again. "Are you all right, Lucinda? You look worn to a thread."

His gruff voice held just a hint of the old Wynmalen, and Elizabeth's eyes were alight as she looked eagerly up from tucking the carriage robe about her sister. But she could see no trace of her dear friend in the face of the man opposite her, and the light died from her face.

Stern and forbidding he sat, his back to the horses. She could feel his eyes boring into her.

After a pause that lengthened into an eternity, he spoke. "I have no recollection of asking you to be my champion, Miss Chanders." His voice was harsh, and his hands clenched the head of his silver-mounted cane in a murderous grip.

Ignoring the flurry of butterflies taking hasty flight in her middle, Elizabeth raised her chin at him. "There was hardly time for you to ask me, sir. The enemy engaged us too suddenly."

"I believe you named me 'Coward.' And 'Faint Heart.'" He paused and let the moment of silence attenuate between them. "Or am I mistaken, Miss Chanders?" His voice was smoother now. Almost silky . . . and infinitely more fearsome.

Elizabeth clenched her teeth at him and swallowed once before answering. "Those epithets seemed . . . useful . . . at the time, sir."

She was having to choose her words as carefully as she'd had to choose them with her stepfather, though that comparison was somehow odious to her.

She refused to permit her eyes to waver. If he was going to tear her to pieces, then let him do his damnedest. She was not the daughter of one of England's heroes for nothing. She absolutely refused to retreat in the face of his obvious displeasure.

"Am I to suppose, then, that you're waiting for me to thank you for your outrageous behavior?"

Elizabeth was startled by his question. She had acted instinctively, impulsively seeking to shield him against a callous and brutal attack. She hadn't had, nor did she now have, any thought of being thanked for it.

She stared at him without speaking, her lips parted in consternation. How could she answer? She was certain anything she said would loose a barrage of scathing comment from the man opposite her.

Taking care this time not to gulp like a raw recruit, she spoke bravely around the lump in her throat. "I do not do the things I do to be thanked for them, Your Lordship." Her eyes flashed with a moment's rebellion, and she added through tightened lips, "Ever!"

His expression became one of boredom. "Not even passing the salt, Miss Chanders?" He looked out the window, as if this remark had put period to their conversation.

Elizabeth was not so hen-hearted as to permit him to get away with such a ploy. "That sort of thank you is merely a social convention, milord. And you know very well it has nothing to do with this conversation." Her eyes were waiting to challenge his.

Wynmalen's penetrating gaze rested on her face a full minute, then he turned those piercing blue eyes to watch the scene outside the coach window.

So. She had won their brief skirmish. Why in the world had it been a battle between them? Was this yet a new Wynmalen?

The man's personality had more facets than a chameleon had color changes! She sighed. At least in this mood he wasn't the cold and implacable bully he had been in the study at Castle Wynmalen.

Concealing a second sigh, one of heartfelt relief,

Elizabeth pulled her light silk cape closer around her. Suddenly she was very tired, and very cold. But there was just the tiniest ever so slightly triumphant smile on her lips as she snuggled closer to her dozing sister.

Lord Anthony Stayne's hearty greeting met her as she entered the breakfast room. "Well! Good morning! I thought you would surely sleep later after your first ball at Almack's."

Tony smiled as he rose and picked up a second warmed plate from the sideboard. "What will you have?" He gestured toward the laden surface.

"Good morning, Tony." Elizabeth paused in the doorway, the heavy skirt of her riding habit looped over one arm.

He was certainly handsome, this man to whom she was betrothed. Why did he not stir her heart with more than calm feelings of friendship? "Just a little, please. I'm determined to get a ride in before I have to dress for callers. Thank you."

She accepted the plate and fought her generous bottle-green riding skirt one-handed as she let him seat her. "Did you enjoy your evening?"

"Very much. It was awful. Some contralto who insisted on singing just the tiniest bit off-key. But I reminded myself that if I hadn't accompanied Aunt, I'd have had to do the pretty at Almack's, and thus had a marvelous time."

"Merci du compliment, bête."

"Nothing to do with you, I assure you. Never could abide Almack's. All those hopeful mothers pushing their fledglings at you." He shook his head, his face full of awe.

He went around the large table so that he could sit opposite her, his plate heaped with scrambled eggs, sausage, and beef and kidney pie. "I'm sure you and Lucinda were the belles of the ball. And I think I rather resent being called a beast, don't you know."

His golden eyebrows drew down over his light blue eyes in a frown that only increased his handsomeness, and Elizabeth sighed. He turned the hearts of half the girls in England. How fervently she wished he could turn hers!

"I'll try to remember that," she said. " 'Beauty and the Beast' is Jonathan's current favorite bedtime story, you know."

He looked up, his face full of sympathy. "Of course you miss him. I rather think we all do. Even Marc."

She looked up from her plate. "Does he really?"

"I think so."

Gazing at him steadily, she realized that she was probably a very lucky young lady. Tony was an extremely nice young man, one who had regard for the feelings of those around him.

He cared for Jonathan. He'd always been kind and patient with him, and he'd surely be so with his own children someday. While she had no doubt he'd not be a faithful husband—theirs was not a love match, after all—she was certain he would be considerate and discreet. All of this was much more than most young ladies of breeding got in their spouses. So why was she so discontent?

There was a small commotion in the hall. An instant later, the footman threw open the door to admit a slightly disheveled Wynmalen.

His midnight-black hair was tousled, and an unruly lock of it fell down over his forehead. On one well-fitted shoulder of his blue superfine riding coat, there was a fleck of lather. It indicated to country-bred Elizabeth that he had been riding hard this morning, and she desperately wanted to know what had driven him to charge full tilt across the countryside.

His color was high, exercise-born and wind-heightened. It gave sparkle to his intense blue eyes. It emphasized, too, the long scar on his left cheek, making it stand out, vivid white, against his undamaged flesh.

To Elizabeth he had never seemed more handsome.

He came to an abrupt halt when he registered their presence and said stiffly, "Sorry. I'd no idea there would be anyone here so early."

At the sound of his deep voice, time stopped for Elizabeth. And looking at him, so vibrant with life that his masculine presence gloriously filled the whole room, Elizabeth knew, as surely as if she had been told by a choir of God's own angels, why she was not content to marry Tony.

Dazed, she never heard the ensuing brief conversation between the brothers. She could only hope she'd had the courtesy to excuse herself before she rose from her chair and floated, borne by unreality, from the room.

CHAPTER
* NINETEEN

Elizabeth fled to the stables with her guilty self-knowledge. There she found the mount she had requested standing restively, saddled and waiting.

"Thank you, Barnaby." She took the reins and said to the smiling boy, "Would you please ask Mr. Daniels if he could accompany"—she saw the crushed look forming on the boy's face and hastily changed her final word—"us?"

He ran to do her bidding, and a few minutes later Daniels, the Earl's chief London groom, strode toward her.

"I wish to ride to Castle Wynmalen, Daniels, and I think I will feel safer with you, as well as Barnaby, in attendance if you could spare the time."

He touched his forehead, and said, "As you wish, miss. A ride in the country would be mighty welcome."

At that moment an undergroom came up leading a hastily saddled mount. Daniels turned to take the reins from his hands. "Good lad. Now fetch me the pistol from the drawer of the desk in the tack room."

The boy ran to do as he was told, and Elizabeth stood, full of impatience to get away to the country where she could sort out her feelings and get a grip on her rioting emotions. Suddenly she had to see

Jonathan. Had to hold him and tell herself that her duty was to make a secure home for him—reassure herself that she could go through with her marriage to wonderful Tony, while her heart and every blazingly aware part of her being cried out that she loved Wynmalen.

While her tumultuous thoughts shook her to her foundation, the face she showed the world was calm. By a mighty effort of will, she stood quietly and stroked her horse's neck while Daniels gave the orders that would run the stables in his absence.

While she waited, Elizabeth called to the youngest member of the stable staff and sent him to the house to tell Lady Esme of her intentions, and to say that she would be back by late afternoon.

Then Barnaby bent and offered his clasped hands. Elizabeth placed her foot in them, and he threw her lightly into the saddle. The two men mounted their horses while she arranged her skirt, then the three of them were clattering down the cobble-stoned alley to the street.

They made short work of the city streets, thanks to the earliness of the hour and the fact that horses were infinitely more maneuverable than were vehicles. Soon they were cantering along the road leading out of the great city in the direction of Castle Wynmalen.

By leaving the well-traveled roadway and going cross-country, they not only had a more exciting and satisfying ride, but they also cut the better part of an hour off the time of their journey. Part of the time saved was due to the fact that Elizabeth rode neck or nothing, letting her feelings straighten themselves out while she concentrated on getting her mount safely over hedge and stream.

Arriving a little more than two hours later at Castle

Wynmalen slightly breathless with two proud retainers in tow, she was greeted by Stone.

"Miss Elizabeth! How very nice to see you!"

"Thank you, Stone. I'm glad to be here. The closer we came to Castle Wynmalen, the more I became aware of how much I missed it."

Her words and genuine smile brought an answering grin from the stately majordomo. "Would you care for a light repast, miss?"

"Thank you, Stone, that would be wonderful." Then, unable even to wait until she had caught her breath, she demanded of Stone the whereabouts of her half brother.

"He's in the library talking to the Earl, miss."

Her eyes flew open. How in the world could Wynmalen have beaten her here!

Stone smiled at her astonishment. "No, miss. Oh, my, no. His Lordship isn't here. His Lordship's portrait that he used to hide in his study is back from the restorer's. It has been returned to its rightful place in the library, just as Lord Stayne ordered. The tyke has taken to talking to it, betimes."

"Oh, dear. Is he so lonely, then, Stone?"

"Well, miss. He spends a lot of time running with Valiant, riding his pony and talking the ears off the staff." His kind smile took the offense out of his words. Then he sighed and said, "But I do think he misses all of you who went to London."

"We'll come to the family dining room for luncheon, please," she said vaguely as she started toward the library.

"Yes, miss." Stone placed her whip, gloves and riding hat on the console against the wall, and started the long walk toward the kitchens. He could have sent a footman scurrying, but he wanted to be the first one to inform them belowstairs that the young miss had come to visit.

Elizabeth walked to the library deep in thought. There was no footman on duty at the door, and she waved away the one that started hurriedly toward her from his post at the juncture of the two halls. She'd paused just outside the door, her hand on the knob, when she heard Jonathan's voice.

"Papa, I *do* want 'Lizbeth and Luce to hab a good time, but I do wish you could hab 'em think about how very lonesome a little boy can get in such a big house. Jus' every once in a while, don't you know?"

Elizabeth pushed the door open a crack and saw Jonathan seated tailor-fashion in one of the great wing chairs in front of the fireplace. Wynmalen's huge black mastiff sat at attention on the rich Oriental rug beside him.

The dog turned to stare at her, his ears pricking alertly forward, and she put a finger to her lips. For an instant she felt foolish in the extreme, then to her surprise Valiant looked quietly away to the boy again, as if he had understood her gesture. His obedience delighted her.

Slipping into the room, she stood silently watching the boy. Jonathan still looked up at the noble portrait of the Earl of Wynmalen, his earnest face aglow.

Had he transferred the affection in which he held her father's painted image to this portrait of Wynmalen? Both men were portrayed in their regimentals. Had their scarlet coats somehow linked them in his childish mind? It would seem so.

Waves of tenderness flooded her. Sudden tears blurred her vision.

Jonathan's gaze never wavered from the solemn, painted face of Wynmalen. "Are they gonna visit before the summertime? Or do I have to wait *all* that long time to see 'em again? It's nice here, and everybody's very kind. But it's not the same as seeing *them*."

His small voice was so wistful, Elizabeth could bear it no longer. "Jonathan," she said softly.

The child frowned, then looked around as if unsure he had heard his name. "'Lizbeth!" Jonathan exploded from his chair and hurled himself toward her, the dog in quick pursuit. Slamming into her open arms, he deposited them both, laughing and showering kisses, on the polished parquet floor.

After a few moments of Valiant's frantic barking and Jonathan's joyous tears, a moist-eyed Elizabeth held her almost-child at arm's length. She smoothed his tousled hair back from his forehead. Looking him over thoroughly, she said in amazement, "Oh, my, just look at how you've grown!"

"Not really. Have I really?"

"At least an inch! I'm absolutely certain."

He threw himself against her, burying his face in her neck. "Oh, 'Lizbeth, I am *so* very glad to see you!" She could feel his body relax against her, as if some self-commanded tension were draining slowly from it.

She struggled to her feet, hampered by her cumbersome riding skirt and the weight of the clinging child she refused to relinquish even for a moment. "I have ordered luncheon, dear. We shall have a wonderful time eating and talking together. Shall you like that?"

The tension shot back into his small body. "Will you go then?" She hugged him closer and started the long walk to the family dining room.

She had never lied to Jonathan, and she had no intention of ever doing so. "Yes, Jonathan, I shall have to return to town. Tony and I are expected at a reception this evening."

His manful attempt to hide his disappointment tore at her heart. He nodded solemnly. "I understan', you and Tony must do the pretty."

Elizabeth laughed to hear him use the phrase he had obviously learned from his good friend Lord Stayne, Tony, her betrothed. Her thoughts thus turned to him and she thanked God Tony was so fond of Jonathan! She couldn't have borne being parted from the child.

Wynmalen, for all his present fierceness, was fond of Jonathan as well. Elizabeth sighed. Why did she have to think of Marcus?

"I must be let down, 'Lizbeth. I'm getting too heavy for you to carry. 'Sides," he whispered confidentially, "we're coming to the footmen." He squirmed free as she lowered him to the floor, then took her hand, walking beside her. "It's prob'ly a little babyish to hold on to your hand, but I don't care. I want to *feel* you near me."

Elizabeth looked down into his upturned face, shining with love and delight at her presence, and burst out, "Jonathan, how would you like to come back with me to London for a visit?"

While Bess packed for the brief journey to London, Elizabeth and Jonathan laughed their way through their meal. Jonathan was almost hysterical with joy and made silly jokes and funny faces all through the meal to entertain her.

At one point he asked, "Can we take Valiant?"

"No, dear. The city is no place for so large a dog."

"He'll miss me."

"Indeed, I am very sure he will. You're awfully good company for him, I'm certain."

"We're good friends, you know."

"Hmmmm. Well, we shall have to ask the staff to be especially attentive to Valiant while you are away."

Jonathan sat back in his chair, obviously relieved. "Yes, that'll be a good idea."

There was a rustle of skirts, and Bess entered the room. Rising to meet her, Elizabeth embraced her.

Bess stepped back and smiled. "It's nice to see that living in wicked old London hasn't changed you, miss."

"But living here at Castle Wynmalen has certainly changed you, Bess! It has given you a rested, rosy look that I find a vast improvement. It's so *good* to see you again."

"Yes, Miss Elizabeth, I think we all feel better away from Chandering just now." She sent a meaningful look in Jonathan's direction.

Elizabeth nodded and briefly closed her eyes in thankful agreement. When she opened them again, they were full of happiness at the thought of having Jonathan and Bess with her in London. The two women smiled at each other over the child's head.

CHAPTER
* TWENTY

Wynmalen was furious. After greeting Jonathan as kindly as anyone could have wished and sending him up to the nursery with Bess, he icily commanded Elizabeth's presence in the study.

Elizabeth had rather have changed out of her riding habit, and nearly informed him that she would join him after she'd done so. The look on his face told her she'd do better to endure her dirt a little longer.

However, as she stamped ungraciously down the hall behind him, she perversely hoped she would develop an itch—say between her shoulder blades—so that she might rub it against the doorjamb for relief, just as a pig scratches against a post. That would show him!

His Lordship waited until the footman had closed the door quietly after them. Then, his hands locked together behind his broad back, he took a few limping paces away from her and a few back, his head bent to regard his immaculate boot toes as if in fierce concentration.

Elizabeth had seen the pose before. It was one her father had frequently used just before he blasted a trooper for some infraction. She wondered if she should come to attention.

Glaring at her from beneath his brows, Wynmalen

said, "I'm exceedingly disappointed in you, Elizabeth." He gave her a quick glance to see how she received this bit of news.

Elizabeth was amused to see him use parade ground tactics on her. She shifted casually into the military posture of parade rest, and, since his comment didn't call for an answer, she didn't give him one. She'd learned a lot watching her father's troops.

Wynmalen was goaded by her silence into looking at her. He immediately recognized her stance for what it was, and his own pose evaporated in indignation. Locking his jaw against any comment that would give the chit the satisfaction of knowing she had caught him out, he rounded on her. "Why the blazes did you disobey me and bring Jonathan to town? You know very well that it is healthier for him in the country!"

In response to his abandoning his pose, Elizabeth relaxed to a more feminine one as she answered him reasonably. "Sometimes there are other considerations, Marcus." She wished he would be more understanding about this, but that would be her old, dear Wynmalen. This new one seemed dedicated to putting her out of countenance. Ignoring his implacable expression, she continued calmly. "In this case I felt that his unhappiness at being away from all those he loved was the most important one."

Wynmalen's tone matched his expression. "He was well cared for at Castle Wynmalen, was he not?"

"Of course," she relied quietly. "The staff is wonderful, and he had Bess. Even so, when I arrived at Castle Wynmalen, I found him talking to your portrait, telling it how very long we had been gone, and how very much he missed us." She lifted her hands toward him, palms up in a helpless gesture. "So I brought him."

"Just like that." His blue eyes grayed with concern and accusation. "Don't you know there is always an epidemic of some sort among London's children?"

"No, I did not. But it should be a simple thing to keep him away from anyone infectious. I shall see to it that Jonathan is kept safe." She took a step toward him. "You know, of course, this is just a brief visit to break up the length of time we must be separated. And you did promise him he would have several visits, you know." She felt a tiny quiver under her breastbone and knew that she was ready to rage at Wynmalen for so casually forgetting Jonathan. Instead she forced herself to continue quietly. "He isn't come to stay."

Her reminder of his promise to the child irritated him. He had certainly meant to bring Jonathan to London. But that was before he had learned of the particularly virulent fever that was making the rounds of the city—and he damn well refused to be put in the position of explaining his actions, or in this case, lack of them, to a mere female!

Her calm irritated him, too. He'd put good men to rout with his displeasure, and for some perverse reason it angered him that this slip of a girl stood her ground before him, unafraid.

Indeed she even advanced, demanding that he understand her reasoning in this matter. At a loss as to how to handle the situation, he took refuge in surliness and growled, "It's on your head if he comes to any harm from this visit, is that understood?"

Her eyes widened at this thrust, and for an instant he felt like a cad. Then he savagely repressed the feeling and stalked from the room.

As he distanced himself from the only person who just might have been able to tell him, he found himself wondering why the child had been talking to his portrait.

Lucinda and Tony, on hearing that Jonathan had come, lost no time seeking him out. They found him with Bess in the nursery and ordered a feast to celebrate the boy's first visit to London.

By the time Elizabeth had bathed and changed for dinner, they'd made serious inroads in the extravagant collation prepared by Cook. The large silver tray looked more like the aftermath of a battle than a treat.

Elizabeth stood for a moment in the doorway, smiling at the picture they made. Three golden heads, close enough for curls to touch, bent intently over the only object left on the tray that hadn't become a complete casualty—a plate of pastries.

"Which one shall I take?" Jonathan's voice was wistful again. "They all look pashatively yummy, and I am *so* full. I can't eat one of each kind."

Lucinda said, "Positively."

Jonathan said, "Oh, yes."

Tony ignored the shambles made of Lucinda's attempt to teach Jonathan English and said, "Take the apple one. They are always the best. Unless you see a raspberry—or an apricot tart."

Lucinda scowled at him. "For pity's sake, Tony. He asked us to help him choose. Don't confuse him."

"I ain't confusing him. I'm giving him the facts."

"Really? Well, it is better when you are dealing with children not to give them quite so *many* facts!"

Elizabeth clearly saw that it was time for her to "deal with the children," again. Repressing a sigh, she called out an obvious, "Ah, there you are!"

"'Lizbeth! We were wondering if you would ever come!"

She crossed the room to them and stooped to receive a big hug from her half brother, calmly accepting his sticky fingerprints on her fresh gown. "I had to take a bath, you know. After all, I rode *vente à terre* to your rescue, and even for the greatest ladies, that is a grubby piece of work now that summer is almost here."

"Daniel said that you were a top-of-the-trees rider, a reg'lar dab hand. Is that what you mean when you say you rode vaunt at hair?" His blue eyes looked up at her owlishly.

"Yes, dearest, that is what I mean—that I rode quite furiously—as fast as I could without doing injury to our horses, to come to Castle Wynmalen and you. For I have missed you sorely, you know."

Jonathan threw his arms around her again, kissing her resoundingly. "I think that is the most splendiferous thing I ever heard."

Lucinda said, "You mean . . ." She frowned and looked to the others helplessly. "Just what does he mean?"

Tony supplied scornfully. "He means *splendid*, of course."

"How would you know any more than I? It is quite possible that he means something more. The word was very much longer." She frowned, puzzled. She had never been at a loss to translate for Jonathan before.

Jonathan turned toward Lucinda, frowning. "Luce, you know I don't know all my words yet," he complained, disliking this bickering between his sister and his friend. "I'm only four, you know." He looked at her peevishly. "I rather think Tony's right, though. I think I did mean *splendid*."

"Well, if you really think so." Lucinda gave his words serious consideration. Then she leaned down to him in a conspiratorial manner and murmured in a stage whisper that could have been heard in the next room, "I hate to have Tony right about it, though."

She was rewarded by a hearty laugh from Lord Stayne, and Jonathan's face lightened. Then the party, coming to an end because the first gong sounded for dinner, became feverishly gay. The three original participants were teasing and laughing and making plans to take Jonathan to see the sights of London on the morrow.

Elizabeth smiled automatically, but her thoughts had turned to her wild dash to Jonathan, and to the new emotion that had precipitated it. Wynmalen— Marcus. Aware now that she loved him, she had to face the complications this knowledge added to her life.

When the first full force of her emotions had hit her, they had destroyed at one stroke her usual calm confidence. She had fled to the only uncomplicated love she knew—the child.

It was as if Jonathan were some sort of anchor, keeping the craft of her life from being swept away on the raging tide of her newly discovered love. With this new knowledge of her deep regard for Wynmalen, she could foresee no end of difficulties.

How could she bear his constant presence in their lives after she and Tony were wed? The pain that tore through her at the thought almost made her gasp.

Was this then the life before her? Such pain to be

borne whenever her thoughts turned to Marcus? Would she, in time, be able to come to grips with it? Or would she, as she was now, always be buffeted by the winds of this new and powerful emotion?

She was pulled rudely from her reverie as the second dinner gong sounded. The party was reluctantly ended by the need for the three adults to dress for dinner. Even Elizabeth would have to change again as well, because of the dear, oh so cherished little sticky fingerprints on this gown.

As she walked rapidly away from the nursery after their quickly exchanged kisses and gaily bidden goodnights, Elizabeth wasn't deciding on which new gown to don. She was wondering instead where she would find a deep enough inner reservoir from which to draw the strength she would need to endure seeing Wynmalen, again and again, for the rest of her life.

"You wanted to see me?" Tony's appearance showed no signs of the haste with which his valet had been forced to dress him. Wynmalen knew, however, that he'd had to rush to make time for this meeting in the study. The final dinner gong would sound at any moment, calling the household to the dinner table. But, rush or no, Wynmalen thought his brother looked singularly handsome this evening.

Regarding Tony solemnly, his eyes quietly watchful, Marcus wasted no time getting to the point. He sat on the edge of his desk and unconsciously rubbed his thigh to relieve the pain there. "Tony. I realize I have forced you into this betrothal." He chose his words carefully. "If it is something you find . . . difficult . . . if you want to call it off, I wish that you would tell me truthfully." There! The words were spoken. Now Tony had but to speak to free himself from his commitment.

And to free Elizabeth as well.

Wynmalen waited, holding his breath, for his brother's answer.

But Tony watched his brother's hand as it kneaded the scarred muscle of his thigh and bitterly reflected, not for the first time, on how little he could do to alleviate Marcus's physical pain. It was a matter of great frustration that he could do nothing to help his brother face that particular enemy.

But he could—and was determined to—help him in his endeavors to protect Jonathan and the two girls from Sir Charles Mainwaring. Marc had made that perfectly clear to him. So even though it meant the end of his personal liberty, he had every intention of doing just that.

"I am perfectly happy, Marc." Well, that wasn't completely untrue. He *was* happy with them all here together. "Elizabeth's a great girl." That was certainly true. He repeated, "Elizabeth is a great girl, and we rub along well." He took a deep breath for the final plunge. "Pray don't trouble your head on that score."

"Thank you," Wynmalen said gravely, and rose, heavy hearted. He stood statue still for a moment, accepting this all but unbearable pain.

It was inevitable that his brother would misunderstand. Heaven knew Tony had seen that suffering look often enough through Marc's long convalescence. Suddenly a weight lifted from his heart, and he was glad he had sacrificed his bachelorhood to bring Marc relief in at least this one area of his life.

Wynmalen threw his arm around his brother's shoulders. "I am . . . relieved"—he couldn't force himself to say that he was glad—"to hear you are happy." And the two left the study as the gong sounded for the third and final time, calling them to the table.

As they walked to the dining room, Wynmalen felt anything but relieved to hear that his brother was so happy to marry Elizabeth Chanders—and he wasn't wondering why!

Chapter
❋ Twenty-one

The whole house was in an uproar. Wynmalen had been looking like a thundercloud all afternoon—again. The entire household knew he strongly disapproved of taking Jonathan out in crowds.

Tony thought his concern was a trifle excessive. Lucinda thought him a spoilsport. And Elizabeth—especially on this day—worried that Wynmalen might have a point!

Now it was time to leave for Vauxhall Gardens, and Lucinda and Tony weren't back from their excursion to Astley's Amphitheatre with Jonathan.

The Earl maintained that a boy unused to contact with other than the country folk among whom he had grown up might be easily susceptible to city illness. His anxiety had conveyed itself to the servants, and the house had a ragged, restless feeling about it that did nothing to help Elizabeth overcome her own fears for Jonathan. How was she to prepare herself for an evening to be spent in Wynmalen's company, she simply didn't know.

"Where in blazes could they be?" Wynmalen demanded of her as he limped into the drawing room.

"I . . ."

There was a hubbub in the hall. They both hurried

out of the drawing room to see that the miscreants were safely home.

Tony smiled a tight smile and came to meet them. Lucinda, a lagging Jonathan at her side, rushed up the stairs.

Holding tight to Jonathan's hand, Lucinda called back over her shoulder, "I'll only be a few moments. I want to settle Jonathan with Bess before I change, but I'll be quick."

Tony called to her to get cracking and received assurance that her maid never failed to beat his valet for speed in turning out her charge. Tony scowled, not caring for the truth of her statement, then turned to the two waiting to explain his party's tardiness. "We stopped by Harley Street. That's why we're a little late."

Elizabeth cried, "Why? What has happened?" Doctors leapt to mind when one heard mention of Harley Street.

"Nothing's happened, Elizabeth. Lucinda just grew concerned when Jonathan seemed a little listless at the circus. We decided it wouldn't hurt to have him looked over." He said to his brother, "You've made us all nervous, you see, Marcus."

Elizabeth heard Wynmalen as through a haze. "Well?" he demanded gruffly. She held her breath, already gathering her skirts to rush up the stairs to check on her beloved Jonathan. She waited only for Tony's reply.

"Jacobs thinks we've been overdoing the sightseeing a bit. Thinks the boy should spend a few days at home resting. That's all."

Wynmalen placed a hand on Elizabeth's shoulder. "Fine," he told Tony. To Elizabeth he said bracingly, "The boy's in good hands, Elizabeth. No need to frighten him half to death with the look you have on your face. If Dr. Jacobs has said that he is only worn out, don't borrow trouble."

Tony added, "Marc's right, you know. You look as if the crack of doom had just sounded. Pull yourself together, my dear." He smiled encouragingly. "I'll only be a moment." Then he turned and dashed up the stairs three steps at a time to see his valet.

For just that instant Elizabeth conceived such a dislike for her betrothed that she could have boxed his perfectly formed ears! She couldn't decide whether it was because he made so light of her concern for Jonathan, or because of the way he so easily cleared the stairs in front of his lame brother.

Wynmalen spoke quietly from just beside her. "Would you mind if I didn't join you this evening, my dear?"

His voice was the voice of her old friend, and Elizabeth turned to see him looking up the great staircase after his brother. The stricken, envious look on his face twisted her heart.

Sensations ripped through her like a thunderstorm, shaking her profoundly. She wanted to laugh for joy at having the old Wynmalen back for even an instant. She wanted to kiss the sad longing from his face.

She wanted to throttle her fiancé for putting it there, then resurrect him to thank him for being the catalyst that again brought forth the original Earl of Wynmalen for whom she so yearned.

Shaken like a leaf in the storm of emotion that swept through her, she could only fight the tears of gratitude that threatened to spill from her eyes at the sight of Wynmalen's dear face. For it was devoid at long last of the rigid, cold anger that it had worn since he had been jilted.

* * *

Elizabeth walked the paths of Vauxhall Gardens with Tony and Lucinda as if in a dream. All her thoughts were on Wynmalen. A wild sweet longing pervaded her very being.

Her mind posed questions more important to her than her next breath. Would the mood in which she had left him hold? The rueful, half-apologetic smile he had offered as they parted had set her heart soaring. Was her dearest Marcus finally himself again? Or would she return to Twining House only to have her breathless hopes dashed to the ground by a resumption of the icy demeanor of the past several weeks?

"Elizabeth!" Lucinda's voice was sharp, and she frowned across Tony's chest at her inattentive sister.

Startled out of her thoughts, Elizabeth leaned forward to peer around the snowy folds of Tony's intricately tied cravat. "I'm sorry, dearest, I was woolgathering. What is it you asked?"

Lucinda looked at her sister in exasperation. "Well, I was asking if you weren't looking forward to the fireworks, but after three tries for an answer, I really don't seem to care." Her beautiful face looked like that of a pouting child.

"Now, Poppet—" Tony began in conciliatory tones.

"Anthony Stayne! If you 'Poppet' me one more time," Lucinda warned him with gritted teeth, "I am going to pop you!"

"Well! Why are you in such a pet, Pop . . . er, Lucinda?" Stayne stared at her in amusement.

"Because I have been looking forward to these fireworks all my life, and Elizabeth won't even know when they go off. And as for you, you won't be the least fun, for you are as bored as you can stick!"

"I am not bored. I'm enjoying walking with you in

the lantern light. Oh, and with you, too, Elizabeth," he added perfunctorily.

Lucinda glared up at him, her eyes flashing like lightning. "Tony Stayne, you great block. You must be the most unromantic man I have ever in my life seen. 'Oh, and with you, too, Elizabeth,'" she mimicked. "Dear lord! How glad I am that *I'm* not your betrothed!"

"Not half as glad as I am." The injured Lord Stayne's handsome face was ablaze with anger.

Two women who'd been sauntering along behind them and whose overelaborate clothing proclaimed their profession stopped to stare. One called out, laughing, "If you don't want him, I'll take him, *Poppet!*" And she and her companion began a catalog of Tony's obvious attributes that brought a flush to his cheeks and caused him to herd Elizabeth and Lucinda quickly away.

Marched at some speed up the walkway leading toward the supper pavilions, Elizabeth saw a servant in the Wynmalen livery standing at the head of the walk anxiously searching the crowd.

Breaking away from Tony, she ran toward the man. "What is it?" she demanded without preamble. "Is something wrong at Twining House?"

"Miss! I'm glad to find you. The Earl is looking for you. Please follow me."

Elizabeth hung close on the man's heels, Lucinda and Tony not far behind. They collected several more footmen along their way, and Elizabeth was breathless by the time the man led her up to Wynmalen.

"Marcus! What is it? What's the matter?"

He took her arm in a comforting grip and drew her close beside him. "That will be all, Mosby. You and the others may return to Twining House now. My thanks to you all, well done.''

Even though blessed relief flowed through Elizabeth because he was here, and he was Wynmalen again and he was safe, she grasped his lapels and demanded, ''Has something happened to Jonathan? Tell me.''

Wynmalen disengaged her trembling hands and looked down into her eyes, his own full of compassion. ''Come,'' was all he said.

CHAPTER

* TWENTY-TWO

His face grave, Dr. Jacobs warned them of the seriousness of Jonathan's condition. "I'm sorry. It must be a very virulent fever to have struck so quickly. I assure you the boy was no more than listless when I examined him earlier."

Then he carefully showed Elizabeth each of the medicines he was leaving for Jonathan and added, "He will require constant nursing. Would you like me to recommend someone?"

"No. Thank you. I shall see to him myself. With Bess to help me, we will manage."

Dr. Jacobs looked closely at her pale, determined face. "If there is a change, or you need me, send for me." He handed Elizabeth the assortment of powders and the bottle of some dark fluid that he had just explained and, ignoring Elizabeth's impatience to be with the child, briefly went over their uses again.

Elizabeth nodded and thanked him. A smile was more than she could manage just now. Finally he left her and she heard Wynmalen's deep, calm voice speaking to the doctor as she turned and reentered Jonathan's room.

Wynmalen called to her as he approached the nursery. "Elizabeth!"

She turned impatiently. "Yes?"

Wynmalen took her by the shoulders. "Elizabeth, you haven't even changed. Go. I'll sit with the boy."

"No, I—"

"Yes." His voice was a concerned caress, wrapping her frayed nerves in velvet.

"You'll call me?" Her own voice was strained.

"Of course. Now go." He faced her toward her room and gave her a gentle push. His eyes dark with worry, he watched her as she moved away, the heavy silk of her dress rustling, then he turned and entered Jonathan's room, where the boy lay, tossing restlessly.

Under the lantern-hung tree branches of Vauxhall Gardens, Lucinda wasn't even attempting to enjoy the evening to which she had looked forward for so long. The fireworks were announced, at last, but she became even more restless. Finally, with a sigh of some magnitude, she turned to Tony.

"I'm sorry I let them talk us into staying. I really feel I should have gone with Elizabeth."

"Don't fret, Lucinda. Heaven knows there are enough people taking care of the poor lad. Elizabeth knows how much you've looked forward to this display. It would only distress her further to have you miss it." He frowned even as he said the words meant to assuage her conscience.

"I know. But somehow fireworks don't seem very important when people you love are having difficulties."

"Good for you, Poppet!" His brow cleared, and a dazzling smile warmed her.

She turned her face up to his, her eyes entreating. "Would you mind awfully taking me home, Tony?"

"Not a bit." His Poppet was growing up, and that knowledge lifted his spirits. "Wait here—Lady Ent-

whistle's party is just over there." He nodded in the
Lady's direction. "I won't introduce you, she talks
forever. Just stay next to them while I send for the
carriage." He turned and moved quickly away,
adroitly threading his way through the crowd of
merrymakers toward the entrance.

Lucinda dutifully stood near the party he had
indicated until a buck escorting one of the Entwhistle
girls began eyeing her in an enthusiastic fashion.
Uncomfortable, she stepped back into the shadows at
the edge of the path and kept close watch for Tony's
return.

Suddenly the shadows behind her stirred. A hand
clamped over her mouth even as she opened it to utter
a startled cry. Her attacker's other arm snaked around
her waist, and she was lifted and borne back into the
heavier shadows and swiftly away.

Struggling fiercely, Lucinda kicked and scratched.
Thrashing as hard as she could, she fought to free
herself of the hand that sealed her lips and kept her
from crying out.

She wasn't terrified. She knew the gardens were
teeming with people, and there was little likelihood
that she would come to harm. If she hadn't been so
angry, she would probably have worried about the
damage to her reputation this escapade might cause.
But she was angry.

Her captor halted and drew from his pocket a silken
scarf with which he sought to bind her hands. Since he
needed both hands free to accomplish this, Lucinda,
her mouth uncovered, threw back her head and gave
vent to a bloodcurdling screech.

An instant later, Tony hurdled into the small clear-
ing in which she and her masked attacker struggled
and smashed a fist into the man's jaw. After a swift

glance to ensure that her assailant was unconscious, Tony swept Lucinda into his arms.

"Oh, my darling," he breathed as he rained kisses upon her brow. "Are you hurt?" He knew she had no knowledge of what could have befallen her and was grateful he had been in time.

Lucinda, so brave a moment ago when there was a need to be, turned into a watering pot now that she was safe in the arms of her rescuer. "Oh, Tony, thank heavens you are here."

"Travers said he had noticed you from his place in the Entwhistle group and was able to give me a point in the right direction." He smoothed her curls tenderly.

"My poor darling. He didn't know you were in peril. He thought you'd moved off because he was admiring you."

Clinging tightly to Tony's broad shoulders, she lifted tear-drenched eyes to his anxious blue ones and became acutely aware that the problem she had just been experiencing was nothing to the one facing them both right now. How *could* fate be so cruel as to decree that they love each other?

"Oh, Tony . . ." She sighed softly just before his lips came down on her own. Neither noticed the escape of her assailant.

The light in the sickroom came from a single candle, as any stronger illumination seemed to cause Jonathan discomfort. By its brave, tiny flame his face seemed so still that Elizabeth found it necessary to touch him at frequent intervals to reassure herself.

Wynmalen, from his chair on the other side of the narrow cot, watched her and mentally cursed the fact that he could do nothing to help.

He and Elizabeth had been at the boy's bedside since he had retrieved her from Vauxhall Gardens. Three of them kept vigil, for Bess, too, refused to leave her young charge.

Elizabeth looked away from the child's face as the door opened and one of the footmen entered, a large bowl of water in his hands. Behind him a maid carried an armload of freshly laundered napkins. Elizabeth smiled wanly and gestured the footman to the table beside her.

When the two servants had withdrawn, she took one of the crisp linen napkins, soaked it in the bowl, and, after wringing it almost dry, placed it lovingly on the boy's forehead.

She looked at Wynmalen. How she wished he would retire. He looked so drawn, sitting there in his open-throated white shirt. She was glad that at least she'd prevailed upon him to discard coat and cravat, for she herself was overwarm in a light muslin gown. Bess was afraid of drafts while Jonathan was so fevered, and the room was stifling.

"Marcus?" she said softly.

"My dear?"

"I wish you would go and rest."

"I have no desire to leave you, Elizabeth."

She looked up from smoothing Jonathan's hair back from his burning forehead. Wynmalen's eyes were dark with an emotion she refused to let herself read. Her heart was no doubt playing tricks on her eyes, to have her see such depth of feeling in the eyes of the man she loved.

He could not love her. He had betrothed her to his own brother. In honor he could not love her. But, oh, how her very soul cried out for him to do so!

A woman's honor, it would seem, stopped some-

where short of a man's when it came to her heart's
deepest, dearest desire. She wasn't aware that she
sighed.

She tore her eyes away from his dear face, then
away from the strong column of his throat to which
she had lowered her gaze. Had the pulse she saw there
really quickened under her regard?

Dearest God! Why must she torture herself so?
Obviously the intense worry over her brother had
unhinged her. Surely she would not have let her heart
peep from her eyes even for that brief instant if she
were not exhausted.

She reached for yet another square of linen. After
soaking it and wringing it out, she exchanged it for the
one that had so quickly become warm on Jonathan's
forehead. Firmly she stayed her mind on the boy,
carefully keeping her gaze away from the handsome
man across the bed from her. Frantically she forbade
herself to love him—desperately she strove to hold
back the tears that had rushed to fill her eyes.

Wynmalen, seemingly at his ease in the deep chair
beside the bed, watched the play of emotions on
Elizabeth's face. Dear gallant girl, she was on the
verge of collapse, but she would not relinquish care of
the boy to one of his army of servants—nor even to the
boy's beloved Bess.

His muscles ached from the effort he had found
necessary to keep himself seated when Elizabeth
had looked into his eyes. He knew his love for her had
been there for her to see—the love he was honor-
bound never to express but was helpless to dismiss.
Surely she had read it there, just as he had seen her
love for him in hers the instant before. His heart had
tried to leap from his chest when he saw the light that
had shone from her face before she'd turned away.

She knew. She knew he loved her!

He bit back a groan. Never had he experienced pain like this he felt at knowing that she loved him and that he had let her discover the depth of his own feelings for her.

Not even his terrible leg wound at its worst could compare with the raging agony that swept through him to acknowledge his love for his brother's soon-to-be wife.

He turned his face toward the shadows until he had gained some mastery over the pain that tore at him. Not his—but his *brother's* wife. How in the name of God was he to bear it?

"Oh, Tony. How shall I bear it?" Lucinda sobbed against his chest in the comforting dark of the carriage. "I shall never wed, so I shall be at home with you and dear Elizabeth, and . . ." The rest of her words were lost as she pressed her face miserably into his now damp shirtfront.

Lord Anthony Stayne stared unseeingly ahead, stroking his beloved's curls. All his life he had played fast and loose with the feelings of the women he had allowed into his life, so perhaps this was some sort of grim retribution for him. But how could this be fair to the lovely girl he held in his arms? She had never hurt anyone, and now she was destined to share the pain of his punishment. His soul twisted at the thought.

"Ah, Poppet." His voice was harsh with longing. "We must be brave, dearest. Fate has indeed dealt us a cruel blow in permitting us such happiness only to snatch it away."

Lucinda pulled from his arms. "Tony! You sound like a hero from some tragedy. We have only to tell Elizabeth. . . ." She stopped, consternated. Hadn't

Elizabeth assured her time and again that she was *happy* to be betrothed to Tony? Hadn't she described how *happy* they would all be? Lucinda looked into her love's face with an expression akin to horror. "Oh, dearest. They must never know."

Tony remembered his brother's arm around his shoulders that night in the study. The night he had taken onto these very shoulders the burden of marriage to Elizabeth. He had done it in order to lighten the load his brother bore. He could never renege on his promise. Never would he deny Marcus the first real help he had ever been in a position to offer.

He sighed. In tragic tones he said, "You are right, my love. They must never know." There was a moisture in his own eyes as his arms enfolded the slender body of his weeping beloved.

CHAPTER

✳ TWENTY-THREE

"How shall I bear it?" Elizabeth looked up at Wynmalen through her tears and begged him to give her an answer she could cling to. She couldn't part with Jonathan. She couldn't. She was so overset that she forgot herself so far as to clasp both his hands pleadingly in her own.

Her touch sent shocks through him. He looked into her lovely gray eyes, deep pools aswim with tears, and cursed himself for a helpless fool. Why must this blow fall now, when the boy was barely recovering! Hadn't Elizabeth had enough heartache?

He had no answer for her. There was none. If Mainwaring wanted to come for his son—and his message plainly stated that he intended to "recover his property from the Earl of Wynmalen"—there was nothing Marcus could do to stop him.

Elizabeth bent gracefully to pick up the letter Wynmalen had dropped when she'd reached for his hands. The letter he'd come to the morning room to read to her. The letter that threatened to take Jonathan from her.

As she straightened, their eyes met, and he placed a comforting arm around her shoulders. Elizabeth turned to lay her cheek against his chest, and he stood quietly, willing his own strength into her suddenly fragile frame.

"We'll fight this, Elizabeth. Don't give up now, my brave girl."

He led her gently toward the settee in front of the fireplace and sat close beside her as she stared into the fire.

"I was such a fool, wasn't I, Marcus? Thinking I would simply flee to you and live happily ever after. Like some threatened princess in a fairy tale. What a goose I was. And I have involved you. I am so sorry."

"I wouldn't have missed it for the world," he murmured. And it was true. He wouldn't have missed knowing her for the world. All the pain in knowing she would never be his and all the frustration in knowing he himself had set her beyond his reach were a small price to pay for knowing her.

This wonderful girl was everything he had hoped for in a woman. All the things he'd lately been led to decide no longer existed in her fair sex. She had restored the deep faith he'd learned at his mother's knee, and he would love her forever for it.

"I would simply flee to you and live happily ever after." The words rang through him like the reverberations of a great church bell, shaking him to the core.

". . . and live happily ever after." Ah, would to God that it were true! For she had taught him at last what it was really to love, and he wanted only to spend the rest of his life seeing that she lived happily ever after. If only . . .

He cut off his thoughts abruptly—savagely. For all that she was his perfect woman, she was not for him. In the study just the other night with Tony he had made certain of that.

Light footsteps sounded on the parquet in the hall,

and Lady Esme entered in a flurry of skirts. "Marcus. Elizabeth. What has occurred?"

She sailed across the wide expanse of the room toward them, ribbons trailing. "Oh, my dear, you've been crying." She sank to the settee on the other side of Elizabeth and took her hand.

Elizabeth offered her a watery smile. "No, Lady Esme, I fear I am not in the past tense yet." She wiped at two fresh tears with the handkerchief Wynmalen offered to replace her sodden one.

His heart twisted. *My gallant, beloved Elizabeth!* His pride in her knew no bounds as he watched her try to ease the worry his aunt felt at her tears.

Marcus took the opportunity to rise. The effort to comfort Elizabeth as if he were merely her friend was tearing him apart. He was grateful for this interruption—for the chance to escape. For the ability to leave to pursue some means of stopping Mainwaring.

"I shall go to my solicitors." The two women only glanced his way, and with a quick bow he was gone.

Several days passed with no word from Sir Charles. The whole household seemed slowly to exhale its collective breath in relief. Jonathan was nearly well, and Elizabeth's smile had returned, though she watched over the boy closely, lavishing every care not only for his health but for his safety.

Lady Esme thought she was watching to guard against a relapse, but Wynmalen knew she was storing his every gesture in her memory against a time when they might be parted.

That certainly did nothing for his disposition, but as he never even vaguely approached the foul temper he had shown during his days of recovering from Lady Emily's jilt, no one noticed.

Wynmalen, when almost a week had passed, could stand the house no longer. "I'm positive everyone else must feel as I do. We've all been in the house too long. I propose an outing to the theater."

While no one was exactly enthusiastic, everyone agreed it was an excellent idea. A play was chosen, and the next evening all but Lucinda gathered in the drawing room appropriately dressed for the occasion.

"I have the headache and feel so hot and miserable. I hope you will all excuse me from accompanying you. I would really prefer just to rest this evening with a cool cloth on my forehead."

Tony knew she had cried herself into her present state—clinging to him and wishing some kind fate would make it possible for them to declare their love. So he supported her in her decision to remain home, adding only, "Poor Poppet. We shall sorely miss you."

Lord Stayne was struck with guilt to see Elizabeth's quick concern that Lucinda might be coming down with the fever that had laid Jonathan low. "Your eyes look rather tired, just as Jonathan's did. Are you certain you are not ill?"

Lucinda blushed furiously, knowing full well why her eyes looked weak, and they promptly overflowed again as she remembered the scene she had made with Tony on the terrace earlier that afternoon. "No, dearest. I am fine except for this dreadful headache."

Oh, how she hated to lie to Elizabeth! Growing up and falling in love was supposed to be a glorious experience. Why was it proving to be such torture for her? Everything was all tangled and pushed out of proper shape. Her dilemma was enough to give anyone a headache. Life was simply not fair!

She turned and went up to her bedchamber, leaning on her dear sister's solicitous arm. She felt like the filthiest sort of traitor as Elizabeth tucked her into bed. Thinking how much she loved her sister's betrothed gave her such a surfeit of guilt that she began to cry, so she was hard put to convince her loving sister to leave her.

The theater that night was full of their friends, all glad to see them out in society again. All were full of questions about Jonathan and best wishes for his continued recovery.

No one in the party from Twining House really knew what was taking place on the stage—each wrapped in a private agony, but glad, also, to receive the felicitations their friends had offered. It was so easy, when fearing for the life of a dear one, to sink into a feeling of isolation that caused one to forget that others cared.

They had passed the intermission pleasantly assuring their friends that they were ready to pick up the threads of their social obligations again, then had returned to their box. As the house lights dimmed, and the stage brightened, Wynmalen's head groom, Daniels, erupted into the box.

Awed by his surroundings, he kept his lips tightly closed, but the anguish in his round eyes was all that was needed to galvanize the Earl. Wynmalen leapt to his feet so suddenly his chair would have fallen if Tony hadn't saved it. The rest of them saw Daniels's panic.

Then they were all on their feet and pressing toward the door at the back of the box, each suppressing the questions that clamored for expression. Once in the hall with the door to the box closed, Wynmalen demanded, "Speak up, Daniels. What's afoot?"

"Sir Charles Mainwaring, my lord!" Daniels cried. "He come to the house and took—"

Tony's curses cut the man off.

The thought of Jonathan in his father's cruel hands turned their collective blood to ice, and with no thought of decorum they rushed from the theater. Their carriage stood ready at the curb, summoned by the groom who had accompanied Daniels, and they piled into it like a crowd of urchins.

Daniels sprang to the box with the coachman, the groom climbed up behind, and they were flying down the street as fast as the horses could go. Not even Lady Esme protested the tangled tumble such haste precipitated in the interior of the vehicle.

Within minutes they were home, the horses' iron-shod feet slithering to a jarring halt before the tall house. The passengers spilled out with a shocking lack of ceremony—stopped as though they had run into a solid wall—and stood transfixed.

On the landing at the top of the stairs, visibly ruffled, stood the Earl's butler, Beamish, a sobbing Bess at his side. And in Bess's comforting arms, as tearful in his distress as was his nurse, they saw Jonathan.

CHAPTER

✳ TWENTY-FOUR

"Matthews"—he pointed to the groom who'd accompanied Daniels to the theater—"my racing curricle! The grays!" he answered before the man could ask which horses to harness. "Beamish," he snapped a second order, "my dueling pistols. And make haste!"

Even as he spoke, Wynmalen was escorting the ladies to the drawing room. "Bess," he ordered her forward. "Quickly, tell us exactly what happened."

Beamish ran into the room and Wynmalen accepted the case containing his matched pair of Manton pistols. With a swift nod to Bess to begin, he set himself to checking their priming.

Bess stood wringing her hands, watching Jonathan where he sat in Elizabeth's lap, crushing her elegant evening gown and crying raggedly into her neck. His tiny hands were clenched tightly in her hair.

Elizabeth, rocking him gently by swaying her body back and forth on the edge of the chair she occupied, looked wide-eyed to Wynmalen even as she crooned soothing endearments to the child.

Bess began to relate the night's excitement, Wynmalen listening closely, his eyes murderous. But Elizabeth had ears only for what the child had suffered.

"Oh, 'Lizbeth, it was him—the awful man from

Chandrim." Elizabeth closed her eyes at the pain of hearing the child so describe his own father. "He came in and he was yelling awful loud about you and about Marcus." Jonathan gulped convulsively and went on. "He said if you were here he would hab killed you both. For . . . coming . . . for coming 'tween him and his true luv."

Elizabeth's face blanched and the look in her eyes as they sought Wynmalen's tore him apart inside. Now then were their greatest fears realized: Elizabeth's in that her stepfather did, indeed, look improperly on her sister; his in that he was certain the man had slipped over the edge of madness.

"Rogers!" he bellowed for his private secretary. His eyes never left Elizabeth's.

"Here, sir!" Rogers stepped out of the crowd of staff that had gathered anxiously at the door of the drawing room.

"A purse. A heavy one. Lots of half-crowns—I'll need them to reward informants as we track them.

"Beamish! Arm six grooms. Daniels! A coach and four to carry 'em. If Mainwaring has henchmen, we'll be ready for 'em."

"Yes, sir, Your Lordship!" Daniels ran from the room to implement the Earl's orders. Tony, recovering from the terrible shock that had until now immobilized him, was hard on his heels.

Elizabeth, having calmed Jonathan to the point she dared return him to Bess, moved to Wynmalen's side. "I'm coming with you."

"No!"

"Yes. Or I ride alone." She spoke very calmly.

One look at the tender determination in her face and he knew he could not deny her. God grant, however, that Lucinda would have suffered no outrage that would necessitate a woman's care.

His sensibilities revolted at the thought of the girl in the hands of a maniac who thought her to be his dead wife.

Mainwaring believed that his wife—now in his unstable mind Lucinda—had deserted him and fled to Wynmalen. The revenge he threatened had chilled Bess's heart more surely than the pistol he'd waved about.

The thought of what could befall Lucinda in the clutches of her mad stepfather chilled Wynmalen's own heart. He breathed a prayer of thanks that Elizabeth had been comforting the boy and had not heard what Bess had had to say.

They rushed out the front door, Elizabeth's abigail and Wynmalen's valet running with them to wrap them in warmer cloaks for the night chase.

Rogers ran from the house an instant later, holding out a heavy purse. Wynmalen accepted it and tossed the purse to Elizabeth, reaching for his driving whip. Before he could even unlimber it, Tony charged out of the alley on one of Wynmalen's prize racehorses. Barely under control, the animal was forced up beside the curricle.

"Hurry! Dammit, Marcus, they've an hour's start by now!" His eyes looked wild in the light of the parish lamps that lined the square.

"Less than that, I think, Tony. We'll catch up to them, never fear." With that he gave his horses the office to start, and the light, two-wheeled vehicle swept forward. They were off!

Clattering through the almost deserted streets of the great city, Wynmalen drove to the inch, nursing all

possible speed from his horses. Twice he stopped and
queried first a lamplighter, then one of the watch.

Each man caught the half-crown Wynmalen flung at
him in reward for the information that a closed
carriage had passed half an hour earlier. Wynmalen
sent his horses furiously toward the post road leading
away in the general direction of Chandering.

Elizabeth touched his arm. "Have you a reason for
choosing this direction? How can you be sure he won't
try for a ship? He would only to have turned off back
there to reach the river."

Wynmalen opened his lips to answer, then clamped
them shut.

"There's something you don't want me to know.
What is it?" Her fingers bit into the firm muscle of his
arm.

Responding to the panic in her voice, Wynmalen
answered reluctantly. "Wounded animals always
make for their den." He didn't insult her intelligence
by saying more. Elizabeth knew that her stepfather
was grievously wounded in his mind.

She didn't reply, but he felt her body move closer to
his own as if seeking comfort. Only the fact that he
needed both hands to guide the galloping horses kept
him from snatching her into his arms.

They were making good time now, the streets of
London falling well behind. Before long they saw a
man trying to mend the trace one of his horses had
evidently snapped. Wynmalen drew his own cattle to
a halt beside the disabled carriage.

"Your pardon. Have you been here long?"

"Long enough." The man's voice was exasperated.

"Have you seen a vehicle with two occupants pass
this way?"

"Not much traffic at this hour, but there was a

closed coach with a man driving someone. If you ask me the driver was demented—it passed about twenty or so minutes ago."

"My thanks!" The coach with his armed grooms caught up to them just then. "I leave a groom to aid you," Wynmalen called to the man.

The wayfarer brightened perceptibly. "Thank *you*." He watched in amazement as Daniels ordered one of his men from the coach, relieving him of the pistol he clutched.

Wynmalen nodded his acceptance of the man's thanks and drove on, keeping his horses to a working trot to rest them. He was less pressured by anxiety now that he was certain of Mainwaring's route and knew he was no longer even half an hour behind him.

Tony, however, could contain himself no longer. He gave the excited horse under him its head, bent low in his saddle, and bolted off down the road ahead of them.

Grimly Wynmalen keep his pair to a measured trot, nursing their energies against the chance that he might have need of their speed later. He could feel Elizabeth's impatience.

Shooting her a glance, he saw her smile her understanding at him. Her eyes conveyed that she knew he must rest the team, even as her quivering lips betrayed the effort she made not to beg him to spring them.

What a marvelous, brave girl she was. How was he going to live the rest of his life without her? His heart twisted at the very thought of trying.

Turning his attention back to the horses, he remembered Mainwaring had a pistol. His thought centered icily on that weapon. With any luck, maybe he wouldn't have to worry about how to live without her.

CHAPTER
* TWENTY-FIVE

Lucinda clung to the coach strap, terrified. All the gay confidence she had gained from association with the loving people at Castle Wynmalen was gone as if it had never been. She was frightened again.

Frightened. Just as she had been whenever her stepfather was present at Chandering. Now, having heard his wild denunciations at Twining House, she was more than merely frightened, she was terrified.

What did he mean, wife? Her mind scrambled away from the thought like some small wild thing trapped in a cage. Did he truly think that she was her mother? That she, Lucinda, was his wife?

She couldn't get her mind to accept the thought. She *daren't* accept the thought—even though he had clearly called her Jessica, and threatened her, as Jessica, with dire retribution for her unfaithfulness in leaving him for Wynmalen.

She was determined to believe this was some complicated game of revenge he was playing in retaliation for their taking Jonathan from him. If she accepted any other reason for his behavior, she would be even more afraid. To acknowledge as fact that he truly thought she was her mother was to admit that she was in the clutches of a madman.

The coach jolted and swayed crazily, swerving from

verge to verge as it was driven beyond safety, beyond sense. Lucinda could hear her stepfather shouting at the horses to increase their speed, and braced herself for the wreck she knew was inevitable.

Then, above the rattle of the vehicle and the pounding of the horses' hooves, Lucinda thought she heard a rider overtaking them.

Then the rider shouted, "Hold hard, Mainwaring!" Lucinda recognized Tony's voice. "Stop that damned coach or I'll blow your blasted head off!"

Horses screamed and the coach tilted crazily as Sir Charles threw his whole weight back against the reins, tearing the horses' tender mouths, wrenching their fragile lower jaws in a murderous effort to bring the vehicle to an immediate stop. "Wynmalen!" he cried in triumph.

Tony ran his overexcited horse against the door of the coach, reached down for the handle, and wrested the door open. "Not Wynmalen, Sir Charles. The nearest thing. It's Stayne, you looby."

To Lucinda he said, "Has he hurt you? Are you all right?"

Leaning down from his horse to assist Lucinda from the dark interior in which fear and the speed of their passage had kept her prisoner, Tony smiled. To Lucinda it was as if the sun had come out.

Sir Charles saw the radiant response on Lucinda's face and was driven to murderous rage by insane jealousy. "Die, Wynmalen!" he shrieked as he pointed his pistol at Tony and pulled the trigger.

Tony swayed slightly atop his mount as he took the ball in his upper arm. He clapped his other hand to the wound. "Not Wynmalen, you idiot! Stayne! You can't even shoot the right man!" he gasped.

Lucinda screamed as she threw herself from the

coach to stretch up and clasp Tony's knee. "My darling, you're bleeding. You're bleeding, Tony."

"You're right about that, Poppet." Tony looked at her dazedly a moment, then slid half-swooning down to where she stood. She threw her arms around him to help him stay on his feet.

Above them on the box of the coach, Sir Charles stealthily drew his second pistol and took careful aim.

Wynmalen and Elizabeth heard the shot. Cursing as if he himself were unhinged, Wynmalen lay into his horses with his whip. The horses responded with an enormous burst of speed. Never in their lives had they felt the whip used in more than a flick, and they ran as fast as they could, frantic to escape a second taste.

Elizabeth clutched at the seat tightly to hold herself in place. Never had she been driven so fast. Tendrils of hair escaped and flew around her face as she hung on for dear life.

Pounding around the next curve, they came upon a scene Elizabeth would remember forever in her nightmares. Lucinda stood beside a closed carriage with an arm around Tony, who was bleeding copiously from a wound in his upper arm. She was trying to lead him to sit on the let-down steps of the coach. And above their unwary heads Sir Charles Mainwaring, his face malevolent, was sighting carefully down the long barrel of his pistol to Tony's head.

Wynmalen tore his own pistol from his belt and fired.

A look of surprise replaced the malice on Sir Charles's debauched face. He half-rose, then folded slowly at the waist and plummeted, dead, to the ground.

Wynmalen's small army of grooms, Daniels and Matthews at their head, was now upon them, and several ran to attend Mainwaring's plunging horses. Daniels himself took charge of the Earl's team as Wynmalen and Elizabeth leapt down from the curricle and hastened to Tony's side.

Lucinda was sobbing, her emotions overborne by the fright she had experienced, her nerves overset by the sight of Tony's blood. She was clumsily attempting to bind up his arm with his cravat while she quaveringly declared her undying love for all to hear.

Tony looked ruefully at his brother, threw his good arm around Lucinda's trembling frame, and said, "Sorry, Elizabeth." He glanced at her like a guilty schoolboy.

Elizabeth looked from one to the other with a radiant face. "It's quite all right, Tony. Really it is." She managed quietly. "In fact, it's quite wonderful. My blessings to you both."

She carefully guarded herself from looking in Wynmalen's direction. How would he take the news that she was free? Longing to know, she was nevertheless afraid to see.

Wynmalen, for his part, hid the exultation he felt and forced himself to go about the business of directing his men. The abused horses were unhitched and the bits slipped out of their torn mouths. Quietly he assigned a groom to each, with instructions to take all four to the nearest inn and care for them until they were completely over their brutal experience.

The grooms, each of them excited to be armed in case of a confrontation with Mainwaring's men— should he have had any—were both disappointed and relieved to be given the familiar job of caring for horses. They moved off in the direction they had come, leading the maltreated team soothingly to a safe rest. Matthews, wearing his newfound prominence well, as he led the fourth horse, directed them.

Then, and only then, did Wynmalen turn to the matter of Sir Charles Mainwaring's mortal remains. He stood staring down at the body for a moment. "Poor devil," he said under his breath. Then, "Duggan. Beck," he called a pair of his grooms. "The two of you put him in his coach and wait with him until fresh horses can be sent from the inn."

He crossed to where Elizabeth was tightening the bandage on Tony's arm. His face somber, he said, "I propose we take the coach the grooms came in and get you to a doctor with all speed, Tony."

Tony nodded, white-faced.

Lucinda burst out, "Oh, hurry! Can't you hurry? Can't you see he's bleeding to death while we just stand here?"

Neither Wynmalen nor Elizabeth answered her. Elizabeth because she knew Lucinda was overwrought, and Wynmalen because in his military career he had seen many a friend bleed to death, and he was certain that Tony was a long way from doing so.

Instead, they helped the young couple into the carriage, settled Tony as comfortably as they could, and asked Daniels to drive back to Twining House as carefully as possible.

Days passed and Elizabeth had not one moment alone with Wynmalen. Days in which Lucinda's radiant happiness and Tony's proprietary contentment as she coddled him became blindingly evident.

Bess went about beaming, delighted that the younger couple had gotten together, leaving the way clear for her dear Miss Elizabeth and the handsome Earl to declare their love for each other.

Beamish had already taken the liberty of informing Stone, his counterpart at Castle Wynmalen, that the field was now clear for their master to pursue the young lady whom the staffs of both households were certain he preferred above all others.

Everyone, after all, knew that Wynmalen loved Elizabeth. It was a subject frequently discussed and rejoiced over in the servants' hall. Everyone knew, and everyone was happy. Except for Elizabeth.

She knew that Wynmalen had to clear up a great many details concerning the death of her stepfather. She knew, too, that he was doing it most meticulously, so there would be no repercussions later. But how she longed to . . . to what?

What if she had misread his eyes in the candlelit sickroom? What if the tenderness she had taken for deep caring was only the abiding kindness that had first attracted her to Wynmalen?

She rose from the bench in the rose garden and paced the sunny terrace. *Could* she be so mistaken?

What would she do if Wynmalen didn't love her? How in heaven's name would she face life without him at her side? Suddenly the long years seemed to stretch out before her like a ceremonial carpet unrolled by an unseen hand to welcome her to her own private hell. And she felt as if she hovered at its edge, on the verge of taking the first step along its path.

She had prayed for a way to be made that would free her from her betrothal to Tony without hurting him, and God had answered with a miracle. A miracle that united Lucinda and Tony. One would think that would be enough for anyone, but no, she wanted something more.

No! That wasn't the truth. She didn't want something more. She wanted *everything* more. She wanted

Marcus Stayne, to have and to hold for the rest of her life.

Suddenly she was weary. More tired than she had ever been in all her days. She leaned back against the sun-warmed stone of the house, and there on the terrace where no one would see, she permitted herself the wonderful luxury of tears.

CHAPTER

❋ TWENTY~SIX

He found her there that evening. He'd been tied up with the authorities over the death of her stepfather and had missed dinner. But he found her on the terrace as soon as he could.

None of the family had known where she'd got to. Which wasn't surprising with Tony making such a fool of himself over Lucinda that Lady Esme did not let the couple out of her sight.

Fortunately for Wynmalen's sanity, Beamish knew exactly where she was. And evidently exactly what she was doing, because the gaze he bent on his master was one of deep reproach.

The old tyrant even escorted the Earl all the way to Elizabeth, opening the door to the terrace himself.

"His Lordship, the Earl of Wynmalen," he announced formally, blocking Wynmalen's view of Elizabeth while he performed this startling act. As he had intended, Elizabeth just had time to wipe the tears from her cheeks before "His Lordship" thrust his butler aside and limped to her side.

Beamish tactfully closed the French doors behind him as he withdrew. Silence so profound that Elizabeth's ears tingled fell on the terrace.

Wynmalen stood three paces from her. She looked so lovely, standing against the wall in the moonlight.

His heart began to pound like a schoolboy's. What had
he to say to her? When he hadn't found her with the
others, his only thought had been to discover her
whereabouts. Now he stood mute before her, wondering what excuse to offer for seeking her out.

"The matter of your stepfather's death has been
settled to the satisfaction of all concerned." Dear God!
Had that stilted tripe come from *his* lips?

Elizabeth denied the lift of her heart at seeing him
and tried to match his casual tone. "I'm glad, Marcus.
Though there is no doubt your brother would have
died at Sir Charles's hand if you hadn't . . . inter-
vened, I am certain you are relieved to have the matter
closed."

"Indeed."

Elizabeth left her place at the wall, the place that
had gently warmed her with the warmth of the sun
caught and held in its stones, while she quietly—and
tearfully—came to grips with her unrequited love.
Moving to the balustrade, she stood looking down the
long, moonlit length of the formal garden.

She heard the unevenness of his footfalls as he
followed her. His limp was pronounced—he must
have stood too long on his wounded leg. How she
wished she had some power over him. She would see
that he rested sufficiently for his leg to heal.

He'd be tired of books and weary of chess, but he'd
be free of pain and able to walk comfortably again if
only she could have sway over him for just a few
months.

But she had just spent several evenings here on the
terrace convincing herself she could live without him.
She mustn't give way to her longings now.

"It did not distress you for my brother to . . .
er . . ." Wynmalen cursed himself for a clumsy fool.

Whatever had driven him in pursuit of her, it wasn't, surely, a desire to humiliate her by calling her jilted. Damn and Blast!

Elizabeth looked up into his guarded face. "Of course not." She smiled in remembrance of the love that shone from the young couple's faces. "I am delighted that they've found each other." She turned back to her contemplation of the garden. "It will be nice, too, to have Tony a part of my family. Jonathan delights in his company, you know."

Unreasoning jealousy surged through him, and words rose in his throat to remind her that it was with *his* portrait that the boy conversed. He was thunderstruck. He knew he loved Elizabeth. There was no doubt in his mind about that. No doubt in the minds of his staff at Twining House, either, he thought wryly. But the child she considered almost her own— was he emotionally bound to him as well? God help him in his decision to renounce his love for Elizabeth. Grant him the strength to carry it through!

For how could he bind a lively family like hers to a cripple? How could he ask *her* to live with a man whose face would frighten her friends?

He turned abruptly away to join her in her pretended contemplation of the garden. It was difficult enough to stand beside her as the light breeze tantalized him with the scent of her. He'd no need to make himself more agonizingly aware of all that was lost to him by drinking in the sight of her as well.

"You will live with them, then?" His voice was deepened by the passions that ran through him.

She turned her head, surprised. "Of course. I can hardly remain here." She smiled at him, her lips stiff with the effort. *I can hardly remain here when you do not love me—will not have me!*

"There is Esme, of course," he ventured, cursing himself for a self-torturing fool. *Ah, yes. Stay in my household. Tear my heart from my body every time I meet you on the stairs—see you across the table. Anything! But don't leave me. Don't leave me.*

Damn, damn, and double damn.

He slammed his hands down on the wide balustrade and braced his weight on them. Elizabeth leaned gracefully forward to look into his face. His eyes were tightly closed, and by the grimace he wore she knew he was in great pain.

"Oh, my darling!" she cried without thinking—without realizing she'd used the endearment. "Your poor leg. How it must pain you!" She slipped her arms around his tense frame and gallantly attempted to relieve him of the burden of some of his weight.

At the touch of her arms, at the press of her slender body against his side, everything in Wynmalen exploded. His love for the girl holding him swept every noble intention away. Passion so long held in check erupted like a flood from the broken dam of his resolution.

Turning in her arms, he grasped her by the shoulders. Ignoring her startled cry, he brought his hungering lips down on hers and kissed her until his senses reeled. Give her up? To hell with the idea of giving her up!

If she wanted to dance, he'd *buy* her a partner. A new one for every waltz—for he'd kill each one at the end of the dance for daring to hold his Elizabeth in his arms!

If his face frightened her friends, to hell with them! He'd so fill her every waking hour that she'd never miss friends!

She was his, by God! She'd been his since the

moment he'd seen her trying to stand up to that bully in the entry hall of the inn.

Blessed inn! He must buy it new stables, at least.

Elizabeth stirred then in his arms, and he released her. She staggered, her knees refusing to help her stand alone, and he smiled, enfolding the dazed girl back into his arms. Tenderly he touched his lips to her forehead.

Elizabeth looked up at him with eyes that were softly out of focus and breathed, "But I thought you didn't love me."

His chuckle rumbled beneath her ear as he held her pressed to his chest. "Marry me, Elizabeth."

She leaned back in his arms to see his face. "You are certain?"

"By God, woman! What would it take to convince you that a man is *certain*?" He stood laughing down at her.

Elizabeth couldn't—didn't want to—take her gaze from his exultant face. She had all she could do not to clutch at his lapels in an effort to keep herself from sliding bonelessly to his feet.

What magic his kisses had worked on her! She was as helpless as a newborn, however far from that innocent state the feelings inundating her senses might be!

"Do you want me to tell you how I nearly drowned in your eyes that day you sat looking up at me from my traveling coach at the inn? Or how very much it has always meant to me that you never minded my disfigurement?"

Elizabeth sighed. "I have never seen you as having one."

For that he kissed her again, until they were both

breathless. He lifted her away from him, setting her on the wide stone balustrade.

"Shall I tell you how dear I thought you when you saved my mother's little vase?"

"I never knew you noticed."

"And do you remember how grim I was in the carriage coming back from Almack's?"

"Yes. You were furious with me."

"Furious, yes. But not with you." Laughing, he said, "Who'd have the courage to be furious with a warrior such as you'd shown yourself to be in your destruction of Lady Emily?"

She frowned at him and shook her head in warning.

He veered away from the subject, serious again. "I was furious with myself for betrothing the only woman I could ever love to my own dear brother," he confessed.

"But I defied you about Jonathan and nearly cost him his life." She was pale at remembering.

"But you nursed him back to health. You never left his side. Never thought of yourself. Elizabeth, I want that kind of caring to be mine for the rest of my life.

"That taste of it I got when you conquered Lady Emily on my behalf and then stood between me and the curious eyes of the *ton* while I recovered from our 'waltz' has whetted an appetite it will take you the rest of your life to appease."

Elizabeth's eyes were deeper and more mysterious here in the moonlight than the fascinated Wynmalen had ever seen them. And full of love.

When she spoke her voice was low and throaty, and he could barely distinguish her words. "All the rest of my life. With you," she said wonderingly.

At that he crushed her to him and kissed her until

the world dropped away from beneath her feet and she heard the stars sing.

"All the rest of *our* lives, my fine, brave, dearest love." *All* the rest of our lives.